CHEESUS
WAS HERE

CHEESUS
WAS HERE

J. C. DAVIS

Sky Pony Press
New York

This is a work of fiction. Names, characters, places, and incidents are from the author's imagination or used fictitiously. Any similarity to real persons, living or dead, is coincidental.

Sky Pony Press books may be purchased in bulk at special discounts for sales promotion, corporate gifts, fund-raising, or educational purposes. Special editions can also be created to specifications. For details, contact the Special Sales Department, Sky Pony Press, 307 West 36th Street, 11th Floor, New York, NY 10018 or info@skyhorsepublishing.com.

Sky Pony® is a registered trademark of Skyhorse Publishing, Inc.®, a Delaware corporation.

Visit our website at www.skyponypress.com.

10 9 8 7 6 5 4 3 2 1

Library of Congress Cataloging-in-Publication Data is available on file.

Cover design by Sammy Yuen

Print ISBN: 978-1-5107-1929-3
Ebook ISBN: 978-1-5107-1930-9

Printed in the United States of America

For my mom, who filled my life with books and taught me that a trip to the bookstore is always the best adventure.

CHAPTER ONE

Miracle on Aisle 4

Every Sunday my town turns into a war zone. On one side, St. Andrew's United Methodist stands poised, huge church-tower bell at the ready. On the other, Holy Cross Baptist prepares to return fire as the choir warms up and the sound system is adjusted. I don't want anything to do with either of them. Me and God, we're not best buds these days.

I shove away from the convenience store's counter, sliding my hands over the nicked orange surface, and count out my cash drawer. This is my first Sunday shift, and after the register is ready I raise a soda cup filled with Dr. Pepper as a toast. It took three weeks of begging and pleading before Ken, the owner, agreed to let me have this shift each week. Completely worth it.

No more hiding in my room and making excuses on Sunday. No more glares from porch-sitting little old ladies. No more lectures about my ungodly ways from PTA moms. They can't fault me for drawing a paycheck. Probably.

Outside, St. Andrew's bell rings, brassy and demanding. In answer, Holy Cross's choir lead, Ellen Martin, belts out the opening bars of a gospel song through speakers wide as a barn door. Minutes later, the bell falls silent and Ellen draws out the last triumphant note of "Hallelujah."

I start laughing. Score one for Reverend Beaudean and Holy Cross. Pastor Bobby's arms must have given out while yanking on the bell pull.

I slip on my neon yellow apron. The words GAS & GUT are scrawled across the top in Sharpie. The store is actually called the Gas & Gullet, which isn't much better. The letters LLE in the store sign were damaged during a storm ten years ago. Ken never bothered to replace them.

My name tag adds an extra layer of tacky to the shop clerk chic. It hangs at an angle, one corner curled forward like a dog's ear. Ken wrote my name, Delaney Delgado, on the front using the same Sharpie as my apron and then slapped a piece of clear packing tape over top to keep the letters from smearing. This town is all class.

Clemency is tiny. Population 1,236. Nora Jean had her baby last week so I'm adding him to the tally. There are only two gas stations, the Gas & Gut and a new Exxon three blocks away. Jobs are scarcer than a business suit on Main Street.

It's a long, slow day. The *buzz-thwap* of a fly beating itself against the front window and the wheezing cough of the ice cream chest provide a steady soundtrack. The AC stuttering to life in fitful bursts adds variety but isn't enough to keep my T-shirt from clinging damply to my skin under the apron. I try to think icy thoughts.

Late in the afternoon, a black SUV pulls up to the gas pump out front and a man in checkered swim trunks and flip-flops gets out. His skin is a red so deep, tomatoes would be envious.

The back door of the SUV opens and two boys tumble out, also in swim trunks and flip-flops. Their sunburns are pale, washed-out reflections of the man's. The first boy, perhaps twelve, leans over and punches his brother

2

on the shoulder, eliciting a yell. The younger boy retaliates with a kick. Their father's hand tightens on the gas pump handle and it looks like he's about to yell. Instead, he reaches over and lightly swats their heads, one after the other, smiling.

While the three of them are distracted, I surreptitiously lift my camera and snap a picture. This is not as easy as it sounds. I don't have the latest palm-size silver toy or a camera phone. My weapon of choice is a clunky Polaroid camera my grandfather gave me two years ago. It might have been new in the eighties when Pops got it, but now it's so battered it looks like it was used as a soccer ball in the World Cup. It's the most beautiful thing in the world.

When the picture pops out of the camera with a soft whirring noise, I yank it free. The boys and their dad are on the move; no time to fan the air and watch the image appear with its own brand of magic. I shove the camera and picture under the counter and straighten up, pasting on my best smile.

"Welcome to the Gas & Gut," I chirp as they come inside. My voice is so chipper, I want to strangle myself with one of the licorice ropes.

The dad gives me a wary look but nods. Within five minutes, they're gone, the boys clutching soda cups large enough to drown in. We should offer free flotation devices with those things.

I pull the photo back out and study it. Exhibit A: portrait of a family, fractured but not broken. Maybe their mom is just busy with her book club today. Or maybe she's five states away shacked up with a boyfriend named Roy. Or maybe she's buried and rotting in the ground. But she's not here. And they're still smiling. Proof that these things can happen. What's the secret? I uncap my Sharpie

3

and label the wide white band at the bottom of the picture with neat, precise letters: MODERN FAMILY.

I add it to my stack of pictures for the day, three deep so far. These are my proofs, my windows on the world. One day I'll be able to line them all up and the world will make sense again.

Just before six, the end of my ten-hour shift, I make a quick check of the aisles and the cold cases.

"Crap."

I forgot to restock the cold case by the register. Andy, the night shift clerk on Sundays, is going to complain about that for a week.

I snag the neon green basket that holds the Babybel cheese wheels. A single cheese remains, red cellophane wrapper bright as a new poker chip. My little sister, Claire, loved the stupid Babybels Mom used to tuck into our lunch boxes. My chest squeezes tight and I pick the cheese wheel up gingerly between two fingers.

"Hey, no bruising the merchandise!" Andy breezes in, his Gas & Gut hat clinging to the back of his head off kilter, shirt untucked, and a cigarette butt still hanging from the corner of his mouth.

I grimace. "Ken will rip you a new one if he sees you smoking in the store."

Andy graduated from Shrenk High last year, but unlike anyone with half a brain cell, he's chosen to stay in Clemency. When I graduate I'll be out of this town so fast I'll leave a sonic boom in my wake.

Andy plucks the cigarette butt out of his mouth and waves it at me. "It's not lit. Ken can't yell at me for a cigarette I've already smoked. Outside. On my own time. Now you," he adds, "won't be so lucky when Ken figures out you're palming the merchandise." He taps a finger

4

against the WE PROSECUTE SHOPLIFTERS sign propped against the cash register.

I flip him off. "I'm paying for it. Don't get your panties in a wad."

Andy grins back. "Sure, Del."

Andy is cute in a middle-America kind of way, with farm-boy blond hair that sticks up in all directions and freckles sprinkled like a dash of cocoa powder across his skin. He's a shameless flirt, but I can't help liking him. Andy works a lot of the night shifts and every now and then we share a shift, though it's rare. The Gas & Gut isn't busy enough to need two clerks.

He catches sight of the empty bins behind me and groans. "Couldn't you at least restock?"

"Yeah, sorry about that. I only just noticed they were out."

Andy sighs, shoving his bangs out of his eyes. "Fine, I'll restock. Beat it, would you? Cindy's coming by later and I don't need extra company."

"You're using the Gas & Gut as a hookup spot? Classy."

"Jealous?" Andy croons. He walks behind the counter and pops the register open, doing a quick count and jotting down the cash total on a grotty old notepad.

"You wish." I weave through the aisles, debating the merits of SpaghettiOs over Beefaroni. I finally grab the Os, a couple stale doughnuts, and a case of Dr. Pepper. Gourmet food all around.

I drop my purchases on the counter in front of Andy and dig in my back pocket for a twenty. Andy swipes the items across the scanner, pausing when he gets to the Babybel.

He glances again at the empty cheese basket.

"I'm sorry, ma'am," he says with mock dismay. "You're not old enough to purchase this without a parent present."

"Hand over the cheese or die." I cock my finger like a gun and scowl at him.

Andy laughs but moves the Babybel to the other side of the counter. "You left me with stocking and you're trying to run out with the last cheese wheel? I need my snacks, Del. This little cheese is payback for giving me extra work. Take your SpaghettiOs and walk."

"That's petty." I drop the crumpled twenty on the counter.

As I grab my change and the thin plastic sack, Andy waves the Babybel cheese tauntingly at me. He's such an idiot. The door sticks when I push it and I curse under my breath, shoving harder. It screeches open. Stupid, cheap-ass Ken never will fix the thing.

"Holy shit," Andy says.

I glance over my shoulder only to find Andy staring down, slack-jawed, at the unwrapped cheese wheel in his hands.

He jerks his head up. "Get back in here! You've got to see this." He puts the cheese wheel down as if it's a live grenade.

What the hell? I abandon my shoving match with the door and head back to the counter. Andy points at the cheese wheel.

There's something weird about the surface of the cheese. I lean closer and then snort, straightening. "Cute. My baby sister used to carve hearts into her cheese wheels too. Except she was five and didn't flip out about it afterward."

Andy looks at me like I'm speaking Swahili. "That's not a heart some kid made and I didn't Ginsu the cheese. It looked like that when I unwrapped it."

6

I tilt my head, raising an eyebrow, and he twists the cheese wheel to face me. I laugh. "Seriously?"

Andy's face flushes red. "It looks like baby Jesus. You see it too, right?"

"It looks a bit like a baby. He's a little lopsided, though." I move, trying a different angle. The folds and indentations of the cheese form a kind of picture, an infant wrapped in swaddling cloths like a tiny nativity piece.

Andy whips out his phone, snapping a picture. "No one's gonna believe this. Holy cheese! Maybe it's like a sign from God or something."

"You think God is talking to you through dairy products?"

"All I know is that is beyond nuts." Andy pauses, fingers poised over his phone while he posts the picture. "Hey, didn't some holy tortilla sell for a couple thousand online a few years ago?"

"No one's going to buy *that*."

"Don't be so sure. This thing could be worth a lot." He pockets his phone and edges the cheese away from me.

"Good luck," I say with a laugh. Sometimes Andy is weird.

I drop my backpack off my shoulder and unzip it, hunting for my camera. I don't have a picture of holy cheese, might be nice to add it to the rest of my collection. Proof that weird stuff happens?

"Mind if I snap a pic?" I hold the camera up for Andy to see.

He covers the cheese wheel with a cupped hand, blocking it from view. "I already sent a picture to my blog. No way you're scooping me on this and posting it to your Facebook."

"It's a Polaroid, genius. Real pictures? Remember those? I'm not going to post pictures of your precious cheese all over the Internet. I want one for my wall."

Andy looks dubious but less likely to bolt. "Just one?"

"Yeah, just one."

"Fine, but you better keep it to yourself." He moves his hand, but stays close enough to snatch the cheese wheel away if I make a move for it.

"You're paranoid. You get that, right?"

"The rest of the world's gone digital, you know."

I hold the camera poised over the cheese wheel and bend to line up the shot in the viewfinder. Moments later, the picture slides free and I watch the image fade into life. "I prefer this, it's more honest. No photo manipulation, filters, or digital crap."

Andy shakes his head, picking the cheese wheel up again and tucking the cellophane around it.

This time, I don't look back when I walk out of the door.

Everybody always thinks they'll know the exact moment their life skips onto another track, the moment the meteor shifts in its path and hurtles toward Earth. I didn't see this meteor coming. Didn't even realize I'd just snapped a picture of it.

CHAPTER TWO

A Family of Ghosts

We live on the other side of town from the Gas & Gut. A few cars pass by as I walk and I wave at the drivers I recognize. They wave back. The sidewalk is cracked and pitted, concrete squares squashed together as though a drunk arranged them. The edges don't line up and if you're not careful, it's easy to trip and do a face-plant. I've walked this way so many times I automatically match my pace to the uneven squares. My own little game of hopscotch right up to our front yard.

In the distance, squat hills and scrubby trees form a backdrop for the town's low buildings—nothing over two stories. Downtown is a child's building block set of mismatched rectangles in competing colors: the bright pink door of Beatrice's beauty parlor in stark contrast to the subdued white concrete of Community Bank sitting next door. In the middle of the town square is a park no bigger than a baseball diamond. A gazebo with peeling white paint perches at its center, and a neglected set of swings and a rusting slide take up the far corner. In summer the entire town swarms that tiny lot for the Watermelon Festival and again in fall for the annual fish fry. Veterans Day will fill the park with old people in uniforms. The town square is the heart of Clemency. Except on Sundays.

Our house is decent by Clemency standards, two stories when most houses in town are one. The yard used to be nice, with wild rosebushes and neatly trimmed hedges lining the front of the house. Now the hedges have turned rogue and attempt to scale the brick walls. The grass was swallowed by weeds two years ago and forms an ankle-deep patchwork of greens and muddy brown. Crossing the tiny front porch, I stomp on drifts of dead leaves. Claire and I used to have leaf fights every fall, flinging fistfuls at each other's faces until our hair was tangled and filled with leafy confetti. I stomp on the leaves harder.

Crickets begin to chirrup and a car drives past, its tires making a soft *shushing* noise against the asphalt. Next door, Mrs. Abernathy's TV is on, and the murmur of voices slips out her open kitchen window and wraps around me.

Inside my house, there's only silence waiting, just like every other night.

I could circle the block a few more times, but the grocery sack is so thin I'm afraid the cans will come tumbling through the bottom any minute.

The front door is barely open when my older brother, Emmet, barges into the hallway. I drop the grocery sack with a shriek. "What the hell?"

Emmet grins, looking way too pleased at having scared the crap out of me.

"Jesus appeared at the Gas & Gut and you didn't call?" he demands.

"Jesus didn't make any doughnut runs while I was on shift," I mutter, dropping my keys into a little blue bowl on the entry table. I ignore the stack of mail sliding off the table edge. I already fished out this month's bills and shoved them under Mom's bedroom door two days ago.

Emmet hasn't changed out of his football uniform and there's a trickle of sweat running down the side of his face. He must have been doing extra drills after the rest of the team packed it in and then run all the way home in his heavy gear. My brother the superjock. High school football is his god. Luckily for him, the rest of the town also loves to worship at the altar of Astroturf. Friday nights are pretty much a high holy day around here and the only time Holy Cross and St. Andrew's declare a temporary cease-fire.

"Heidi texted me five minutes ago. Said she saw something on Andy's blog about Jesus appearing," Emmet says. "I knew that guy was a stoner."

"Since when does Heidi read Andy's blog?" Guess I'm even more out of the social loop than I thought. Also, who still blogs?

Emmet shrugs. "Heidi said Mary called and told her to check it out."

"It's been like twenty minutes. Unbelievable." I don't know why I'm surprised. It's not like there's anything to do in this town except talk about everybody else's business. But even by Clemency's standards, that was fast.

"Are you saying it really happened?"

I shove the grocery sack into Emmet's hand. "Dinner. SpaghettiOs. Fix us both a bowl and I'll tell you all about it."

Emmet glances upstairs, weighing the sack in his hand.

I shake my head. "You know Mom will be out the door any minute."

Emmet's shoulders stiffen and he turns, shuffling into the kitchen with the plastic bag banging against his leg. A few years ago, Mom would never have missed a family dinner. Of course, a few years ago she would have been cooking.

11

I have Claire to thank for the dramatic changes in our family.

After she died, when the silence in the house felt like it might smother me in my sleep, we all went a little crazy. Emmet and I recovered. Our parents didn't. My mom took a night shift at the Everything Store, a Walmart wannabe on the edge of Clemency, and we've hardly seen her since. My dad, a mechanic at Lucky's Lube & Tune, took off one day after yet another fight with Mom. He's in Montana, as far from our screwed-up little family as he can get. It's like we buried our parents with Claire. The result is basically the same.

My eyes are drawn to the family portrait hanging over the entry table. It's three years old, taken at Christmas—the last time we were a normal family. Three months before Claire got sick. Mom's hair had been permed and she looks like a blonde poodle wearing a Santa hat. Dad's glasses are crooked, and both of them have fixed take-the-damn-picture smiles, but Emmet and I are laughing, and Claire's looking sideways because Emmet had just yanked her ponytail. My brother's hair is slicked back with gel, his square face spotted with acne on his chin and cheeks. I look like my dad and brother, same dark hair and eyes, my skin tawny brown. There's no trace of Dad's Mexican heritage in how I was raised, but it's stamped on my face. Claire looks like Mom, with the same blonde hair and sharp cheekbones. Her skin is corpse white compared to the faces around her, though. Maybe that should have been our first clue something was wrong.

We look happy in that picture, normal. But those people are ghosts of a family that no longer exists.

I curse under my breath and move into the kitchen.

Emmet holds an open can over a pink plastic cereal bowl and smacks the bottom. I snatch the can out of his hand and use a fork to knock the last dregs into the bowl. I have mad dinner skills.

"Go on, big guy, take a seat. Wouldn't want you to strain those oh-so-important fullback muscles."

Emmet whaps the back of my head before sitting and propping his legs on the table. I knock his feet down as I pass, smirking when he scowls.

"No shoes on the table. I don't want Astroturf getting in my SpaghettiOs."

"You're not Mom. Stop acting like her." Emmet slaps his heels back onto the table and tips his chair up on two legs.

If I was trying to act like Mom, I'd leave him to starve. Ungrateful bastard.

I kick the closest chair leg and Emmet goes flying backward, hitting the floor hard. He scrambles up and makes a grab for me, but I dance out of reach.

"Uh-uh, wouldn't want to spill dinner, would you?" I hold the bowls over my head and back around the table, sticking my tongue out.

"The moment you put those down, you're toast."

I make sure to keep the table between us and pop the bowls into the microwave. "I thought you wanted to hear about Jesus's miraculous appearance at the Gas & Gut? It's gonna be hard to talk if you're strangling me."

"I'll risk it." Emmet rights his chair and sits, feet on the ground this time, glaring at me. "Why are you in such a good mood?"

I can't tell Emmet it's because he's home and this place doesn't feel like such a tomb when I've got him to bug, so

I shrug and lean back against the counter. "The thing with Andy and the cheese wheel is funny."

I drop our bowls onto the table and as soon as I sit down, Emmet kicks my leg under the table. "What cheese wheel and what's up with Jesus?"

I scowl but explain about the Babybel, expecting him to laugh. Instead, he looks thoughtful.

"That's weird. But cool."

Before I can answer, a door opens then closes upstairs. Emmet and I both go still, looking up at the ceiling. Seconds later there's the soft *thunk* of footsteps on the stairs, the rattle of keys being grabbed from the front table, and the cold, impersonal thud of the front door banging closed.

"Have a nice night! Love you too!" I yell, layering enough sarcasm into the words to strip paint.

"Don't," Emmet mutters.

"Why not?" I snap. "I could stand a foot away from her, yelling, and she'd still be in zombie-Mom mode."

Emmet drags a hand across his face. "Just don't."

The defeat in his voice stops my tirade before I can really get started. We don't talk about Mom just like we don't talk about Claire. I could fill the hall closet with all the things we don't talk about anymore.

He gets up, dumps our empty bowls in the sink, and messes up my hair on his way out of the kitchen. "Thanks for dinner."

"Yeah, yeah." I grip the edge of the counter and stare after him, resisting the urge to apologize for what I said about Mom. We both know I wouldn't mean it.

Sighing, I grab my backpack from the front hall, jog upstairs, and slip into my room.

Home sweet sanctuary.

Walking into my room is like standing in the middle of a kaleidoscope. The walls are covered by hundreds of Polaroid pictures from waist high up to the ceiling, each held in place with a pushpin. If I took them down there'd be so many little holes in the wall you could shine a light through and make a giant star field.

When I first started taking pictures, I wasn't picky about what I shot. I burned through the film packs Pops gave me like they were tissues. As soon as I had to start buying my own Polaroid packs though, I figured out just how much classic film costs. A huge chunk of my paycheck goes to support my photo habit these days.

All those pictures on my wall might look like chaos, but there's a message and a theme in each sweep of images. Beside my bed are the photos that speak of family and friends, of how things should be. That's where I'll add today's snapshot of the sunburned father and his sons.

Beside the closet is my WTF wall, filled with the odd and offbeat. There's a picture of a two-headed snake Mrs. Jasper found in her shed, another of a broken swing with a sparkly pony sticker tacked to the bottom. Andy's cheese wheel will be in perfect company.

When Pops gave me his camera, a year before Claire's death and just months before his own, he told me, "A Polaroid camera's a kind of truth you can't find anywhere else. You press a button and a minute later you're holding a small piece of the world. The image quality might be crap, but so's the world lots of times."

I frown at the grainy image of the cheese wheel, trying to find Pop's truth in it. Andy probably faked the whole thing. Or maybe a factory defect caused the surface of the cheese to warp? Because if God is sending some big message via dairy express, I can't figure out what it is.

Chapter Three

Christening Cheesus

My alarm blares, dragging me out of a dream where my best friend Gabe and I are kissing. We've never crossed the friendship barrier in real life. I'm pretty sure Gabe's never even thought about it. I can't say the same. But here's the thing: He really is my *best* friend. Okay, like my only friend. There's no way I'm going to risk wrecking that by making a move. Unfortunately, my subconscious hasn't gotten the memo. I shake off the dream and roll out of bed.

Emmet takes half an hour to get ready in the mornings. He's a guy; he should be in and out of the bathroom in two minutes. But his routine hasn't varied for over a year. Maybe it really does take him that long to apply hair gel, slap on some cologne, and admire his pecs.

I wait in the car, drumming my fingers on the cracked dashboard and making little holes in the layer of dust. Emmet will be driving, of course. I have my license, but the only spare vehicle is this old Buick my brother bought six months ago. It was cheap because it's the ugliest car ever made—squat and wide with each door a different color and Rust Bucket painted on the hood in foot-high black letters.

I lean over and smack the horn. Rust Bucket belches out a noise like a jet engine being stomped by an elephant.

"Come on, Emmet," I yell out the window. "No one cares if you have a hair out of place. You've got practice after school anyway."

Emmet appears in the front doorway and shoves a last bite of Pop-Tart into his mouth. His right cheek bulges like a hamster's.

"Zip it," Emmet growls, spraying crumbs. The car drops lower as he climbs in.

Rust Bucket shudders to life with a squeal, and black smoke billows from the tailpipe. The ride to school only takes five minutes, seven if all three of the stoplights are against us.

Shrenk High squats on a patch of land at the edge of town. To the right of the school, a low chain-link fence surrounds the sports field and a row of bleachers only five benches high. The field is used for everything from our ten-person track team to the football and soccer teams. Football gets first dibs on practice time, though. Even among extracurriculars there's a pecking order.

On the other side of the school is the tiny parking lot. It has as many potholes as parking spaces and one sad little tree in the middle. The actual school is a cluster of three buildings: the elementary, middle, and high schools. They share a single gymnasium, which usually means we're tripping over the kindergartners' T-ball bats and jump ropes when it's time for our daily PE torture session. There aren't enough kids to merit completely separate schools so the county decided to save money and build this monstrosity. Last year's graduating class, the biggest in the school's history, had sixty-seven students. I've been going to school with the same kids since I was five.

Gabe is waiting for me by the entry doors, back propped against the metal railing that separates the middle school from the high school.

"Morning, Beaudean," I say, pausing to bump my shoulder against his.

"What's up, Delgado?" Gabe smiles.

I try not to focus on Gabe's lips, worried he'll guess about last night's dream. His jeans hang loosely on him and he's grown another few inches over the past months. He's all knees and elbows, his skin tanned the color of burnt summer grass.

Truth is, Gabe and I are odd friends. Under normal circumstances we'd barely talk to each other. But our friendship is anything but normal.

When I was ten, Reverend Beaudean and his family moved to town from Louisiana. Rev B and Gabe were fine, but Gabe's mom, Lila, stirred up all sorts of gossip, especially when she wore her micro miniskirt for a stroll down Main Street. A few months later, Lila shocked the town biddies when she ran off with some trucker passing through. Worse, she stole all the proceeds from the Ladies Auxiliary bake sale before she left.

For weeks, Lila and the missing bake sale money were all anyone could talk about. No one wanted anything to do with Gabe. They couldn't shun Reverend Beaudean— he was a preacher after all—but Gabe was fair game.

I threw my very first punch the day Wayne Hissep called Gabe a gator-hugging swamp baby and accused him of helping Lila steal. Gabe and I weren't friends, but Wayne was way out of line. I skinned my knuckles, bruised Wayne's cheek, and ended up grounded for two weeks.

I also ended up with Gabe as my best friend. You're either born friends in Clemency, or trouble ties you so tight together you don't have any other choice. I'm glad I punched Wayne way back then. Some friends are worth fighting for.

"Earth to Del, hello?" Gabe says, dragging me back into the present. "Why are you looking at me like that?"

I glance away and shrug. Was I staring at his lips again? "Maybe I just think you're weird."

"Please, you're the one who totes around a camera older than the school. How was your first Sunday shift?" Gabe falls into step beside me as we enter the main doors. "Sorry I didn't come by yesterday, I got caught up with helping Dad after the service."

"No worries. You'd have been bored. It was so slow I almost gave Santa a makeover."

The front window of the Gas & Gut features a life-size painting of Santa Claus holding a turkey leg. Ken paid some drifter two cases of beer to paint the figure last November. Now, almost a year later, Santa's paint is cracking and there are scratches in inappropriate places thanks to the middle schoolers. Ken's so proud of that Santa he refuses to clean the front window, but he never said anything about modifying Saint Nick.

Gabe laughs. "What kind of makeover are you planning?"

"Santa needs to get with the locale. I'm thinking a cowboy hat." I change out my books.

Gabe shoves every book he has into his navy backpack, making it bulge. If I press a finger against his shoulder I bet he'll tip over. "Ken'd skin you if you touched Santa," Gabe says.

He has a point. Is alleviating boredom worth my life? Guess I'll have to decide next Sunday.

We head for homeroom. All around us students rush, shoving open lockers, searching for lost assignments, and gossiping about their weekends. The hallway is filled with the dull roar of two hundred kids on the move.

"You're a good artist," Gabe says. "Ken should've paid you to paint the front windows."

I grimace. "I'm not interested in the sort of currency he was offering. Beer isn't my thing." Vodka gets the job done faster, mixes well with lots of stuff, and doesn't taste like you're licking the bottom of a toilet bowl. Too bad I cleaned all the vodka out of Dad's liquor cabinet six months ago.

"True. But if he'd offered you some camera film, I bet you'd have painted the walls, windows, and roof." Gabe slides a sideways grin at me.

"Are you calling me cheap?"

"Nah, just obsessed. Get any new pics?"

"A couple. I snapped one of Andy's holy cheese."

Gabe's eyebrows hit his hairline. "Holy cheese?"

"I can't believe you haven't heard." I edge past him into the room. Homeroom is basically a homework catch-up session and announcement time, so we don't have assigned seats. It's the only time we get to sit together all day, other than lunch. "Emmet knew about the cheese wheel by the time I got off shift. Power of the Internet and all that. Also, did you know Andy has a blog and people actually read it?"

"Can we focus? Why is the cheese holy exactly? Is it a Swiss kinda thing?"

Before I can explain about the cheese wheel, the last warning bell rings and Mrs. Winnacker gets to her feet.

Her frizzy brown hair adds three inches to her five-foot height and thick glasses teeter on the end of her nose, threatening to hit the floor at any moment. She glares and the room falls silent. Mrs. W might be tiny and unimposing, but no one hands out more detentions.

I shrug at Gabe and mouth, "Later."

He nods once, rolls his eyes, and switches his attention to Mrs. Winnacker.

I pull out my worksheets and hideously thick math book. When homeroom ends half an hour later, I feel as though my brain has been squeezed through a pasta strainer. "Who cares what freaking x means anyway? I've never had to make change for a customer and been forced to multiply by x, divide by z, and then quantriple the remainder by a factor of 7." I slam the cover closed on my math book, shove it in my backpack, and get up.

"That's your problem." Gabe puts away his copy of Shakespeare's *Twelfth Night*. "Making change is way more fun if you quantriple it by a remainder of 7."

"We can't all be math geniuses," I mutter. I take perverse satisfaction in watching Gabe struggle with his backpack. He's always been an A student, and while I love him, I also occasionally want to smack him over the head with a protractor and some graph paper.

"I'm glad you recognize my better qualities," Gabe says.

"Sure I can't bribe you into doing my math homework?" I bat my eyelashes and give him a soppy smile.

"Not a chance." Gabe shoves me ahead of him and out of the room. "Come on, you owe me an explanation about holy cheese. Can it make the meatloaf in the cafeteria edible?"

"The pope couldn't do that."

"Still waiting for an explanation."

"It's stupid. Andy unwrapped one of those Babybel cheese wheels, the kind dipped in red wax. The cheese inside had an image sort of stamped or carved into it. Andy says it's baby Jesus, maybe even a message from God, but I'm not feeling it."

Gabe shakes his head. "Probably just something random."

"Probably. I doubt God has anything to say to anyone in Clemency."

"My dad would disagree." Gabe touches the small silver cross he always wears. He's had it as long as I can remember.

"Your dad thinks God communicates through snack food?"

"He quotes that 'God works in mysterious ways' line all the time. I bet he'd buy into the holy cheese story."

"That's all Andy needs, someone credible reinforcing his delusions."

Gabe shifts his backpack and glances at the hall clock. "One minute warning. Better get to math or you'll miss that algebra test. Wish me luck with Shakespeare."

I wave Gabe away. "Fine, go enjoy English while Mr. Sutherland tortures me to death. You're such a sadist."

"You know me so well." He laughs before turning to jog down the hall.

I make it through the classroom door as the bell rings. Everyone else is already seated and Mr. Sutherland is writing a problem set on the whiteboard. The bald spot on the top of his head is shiny under the fluorescent lights and his blue dress shirt is untucked in the back. As he adds the last inscrutable letter to his demonic math example,

Mary leans over to Anna and whispers, "Have you seen the picture on Andy's blog?"

By lunchtime, it's clear that Gabe's ignorance about the cheese wheel is an isolated phenomenon. Andy's blog and the picture he posted dominate school gossip. Half the school thinks the thing is a fake and the other half are willing to admit God might have a dairy fetish.

Gabe is a brown bagger, bringing his lunch each day in a black insulated sack. I, however, rely on the questionable cooking skills of our cafeteria lunch ladies. Which means Gabe is on table stakeout duty while I get to stand in line. I balance my tray one-handed and take my seat beside Gabe.

"Thank goodness Andy left my name off his blog," I say. "Bad enough having everyone ask me if I've heard about Baby Cheesus without them knowing I actually saw the thing in person."

"Baby Cheesus?" Gabe laughs. He's arranged his food in front of him in a semicircle: an egg salad sandwich, small red apple, bag of Fritos, and a peanut butter bar. Gabe goes for the peanut butter bar first. The boy has taste.

"Not sure which genius came up with that name, but it's sticking." I poke a fork at the fried meat patty on my plate and wait to see if it fights back.

Gabe shakes his head. "By tomorrow they'll be talking about how Mrs. Dixon's dog crapped on Mrs. Rutherford's lawn."

"You're probably right."

And everything might have ended there, just as Gabe predicted. Except for Wendy Stevenson.

Chapter Four

Wendy Stevenson's Miracle Cure

Wendy Stevenson is the type of blonde that clichés are built from: model-thin, gorgeous, and head of the social scene. She's rodeo queen of Ballard County and has enough calf-roping trophies to start her own herd. Otherwise perfect in every way, Wendy has one tragic character flaw: she's decided we're besties.

It's not something I'm prepared to forgive.

Standing beside my locker before lunch Tuesday, I watch with fatalistic despair as Wendy bounces down the hall toward me, her million-watt smile in place. Predictably, Wendy stops beside me. I resist the urge to bang my head against my locker.

"Hi!" she trills, standing way too close. Personal space is not something Wendy understands. She pats my arm and smiles. "Want to grab a seat in the caf together?"

"No. Just waiting for Gabe." I back up, bumping into my locker and dislodging Wendy's hand.

"But there's been another miracle. Don't you want to hear all about it?"

Okay, now that kinda grabs my interest. First, when did people start calling Baby Cheesus a miracle? And

25

second, what in the world is Wendy talking about? I mentally file the excuse I was preparing and save it for later. "Another?"

"Yes! It's the most amazing thing." Wendy bounces on the balls of her feet, almost vibrating with excitement. If she launches into full-blown hysteria I'll be forced to slap her. It's what you're supposed to do, right? The fact that I'll enjoy it is entirely beside the point. "You have to let me tell you all about it," Wendy continues. "But not here. The hallways smell like dirty socks."

Sadly, Wendy is right.

"Just the two of us?" I tap my fingers against my leg, remembering the last time I got roped into an unofficial meeting of the blonde brigade while Wendy held court in the cafeteria.

"No, silly, I invited some others too. I can't keep this all to myself, that would be selfish."

Of course it would. I nod glumly. "Trish and Anna?"

"Totes! And Neil and Eric and Wayne and Isabelle and Nancy, of course. Oh, and I think Mary might sit with us as well. It'll be cozy!" Wendy bobs in place, looking gleeful.

"I'm sorry," I blurt out. "I've got to research a paper for Mrs. Morrison's class. I'll be stuck in the library all lunch period."

Wendy wrinkles her nose. "Don't be silly, you have to eat." She grabs my wrist and drags me toward the cafeteria. For five foot nothing, Wendy is strong. Must be all that calf roping.

I splutter and protest, but Wendy is a miniature hurricane in designer jeans. All I can do is surrender and be pulled along in her wake. Just then, Gabe reaches his locker and glances up, startled.

26

"I can't just abandon Gabe," I try.

Wendy glances at Gabe and smiles sweetly. "Gabe doesn't mind. He sits with you every day."

I give Gabe a pleading look. He snickers and turns away, pulling his lunch bag out of his locker.

"I hate you!" I snap at Gabe, leaning close before Wendy gives another tug and I stumble after her.

He waves. "Have fun at lunch!"

After school, I am going to take Rust Bucket and run him over. Twice.

Gabe thinks Wendy's delusions of friendship are hilarious. He's always teasing me about joining the rodeo club and dyeing my hair blonde. All of which means he's no help at all whenever Hurricane Wendy comes to town and drags me into something. I can't figure out if he's secretly afraid of her or easily entertained.

Wendy shoves open the cafeteria door with her shoulder, giving me another small jerk. She pauses in the doorway to make sure everyone is looking before dropping my wrist and sashaying inside. I consider fleeing, but I'm pretty sure Wendy would chase me down.

I have several theories about Wendy's burning need to be friends.

Theory one: alien abduction. Wendy is actually a little green man in disguise, sent here to study and torture innocent high school students.

Theory two: demonic possession. In an effort to boost hell's numbers, Satan is now recruiting popular teen girls and getting them to steal souls.

Theory three, my personal favorite: government experiments gone wrong. Wendy's part of a secret government program to create teen superspies, but her mind snapped, she was kicked out, and now she's batshit crazy.

27

Long, arduous minutes later, after being herded through the lunch line, I slump in my seat at Wendy's usual table, picking at my food.

Of course, I know the truth about Wendy's friendship efforts. But I don't want to admit it, even to myself. Until Claire died, Wendy never showed the slightest interest in me. Wendy is Pastor Bobby's daughter and she takes her role as preacher's kid very seriously. I'm Wendy's charity project. Pastor Bobby probably talked her into it. And Wendy always sticks with anything she sets her mind to. At least once a month, Wendy tries to drag me into hanging out with her and talking about my feelings. I don't share well, feelings or otherwise.

Wendy snaps her fingers in front of my face. "Hello? Did you hear what I said?"

"No, sorry," I mutter.

Wendy sighs and flashes a look at her real best friends, Trish and Anna. Trish is petite with dimples and huge blue eyes, top of the cheerleader pyramid—though not socially, of course. She gets straight As and is working toward a scholarship to Northwestern. Anna, on the other hand, is as annoying and perky as Wendy. They could be twins. Though, to be fair, Wendy is definitely the smarter of the two. Anna skates through life with a C average and a pair of D cups filling out her varsity sweater that have every boy in the school fascinated. Including Gabe, much to my disgust. Anna's boobs clearly have superpowers.

"Pay attention." Wendy thumps my arm and leans in closer. The others all lean in as well. "Yesterday, I had the worst head cold. It was horrible! Snot dripping from my nose, my eyes were red, and I sounded like a bullfrog. So gross. I told Daddy I had to stay home. Now I don't know if you heard, but Daddy bought that cheese wheel from my cousin Andy for fifty dollars and so we prayed over the cheese wheel. It being a holy sign and all."

Wait. Pastor Bobby bought the cheese wheel? I know Andy was yammering about selling it on eBay, but that's a little different from someone local buying the thing. And how'd Bobby settle on fifty dollars? Is there a price guide for bogus religious signs?

"And this morning, when I woke up," Wendy continues, "my head cold was completely gone and my hair looked fantastic."

Unbelievable. The level of stupid at this table just reached epidemic proportions. There's no way anyone's going to take Wendy seriously.

Anna gasps and presses a hand against her chest. I bet she practices that move in the mirror at night. All the boys at the table stare at Anna's chest, transfixed. "I thought your hair looked different today!" Anna says. "It's all wavy."

Wayne tears his gaze away from Anna's breasts and turns to Wendy. "You think Baby Cheesus is a real miracle? That God sent it?"

Wendy nods. "Daddy says that Baby Cheesus is a sign of God's divine hand at work in our little town. That cheese wheel has healing powers. And look at my hair. It has to be God's work."

Everyone at the table is hanging on Wendy's every word. Apparently I was wrong. They *are* taking her seriously.

I snort back a laugh. "God did not give you a makeover." Every eye turns to me and I hold up my hands. "What? I'm just saying there's no way God has switched from burning bushes to curling irons."

Neil Clover nods. "Del's right. I think Andy faked the whole thing. He probably made the cheese wheel hoping someone like your dad would buy it off him, Wendy."

I stare at Neil. He's a rising star on the baseball team, handsome in an offhand way, with ears a bit too big. Part of Wendy's regular crowd, a future ex if he isn't one already. Neil is easy to ignore because he never speaks up. So why's he agreeing with me now?

Wendy's lower lip juts out and she sets her pretty jaw. "God and Baby Cheesus healed me! I might have woken up with pneumonia. My cold was that bad. I might have been in the hospital. This is a genuine miracle!"

Neil falters under Wendy's glare and shrugs. "Okay, okay. The cheese is magic."

Wendy's face flushes. "It's miraculous!"

I hold back another laugh.

"Miraculous," Neil agrees. He turns to Wayne quickly and starts talking about the baseball team's prospects for the upcoming season. Wayne smirks but keeps up his side of the conversation.

Wendy's narrowed eyes swivel to me.

"You believe in Baby Cheesus, right, Del?"

I feel like there's a grenade launcher pointed at my head. Red lights and warning sirens should be blaring all around.

"I need to get in some research time, sorry to eat and run." I leap up, grabbing my backpack and abandoning my barely touched food. Starvation is the safer option. If Wendy has decided Cheesus is miraculous she's not going to let it go.

Wendy scowls and opens her mouth to say something, but Trish interrupts. "Your hair really does look fabulous. I'd kill for waves like that. Maybe you can bring Baby

Cheesus over to my house tonight and we can have a makeover party."

Wendy pats her hair and smiles. I escape before she remembers I'm not a member of the Cheesus pep squad.

I have an hour and a half after school before my shift at the Gas & Gut starts. It's just enough time to head home, grab a snack, jump online, and then change into the black slacks and white shirt I normally wear to work.

I freeze when I enter my room, staring at the bed. The covers are neatly tucked and all three of my pillows are arranged in a demi-pyramid worthy of a magazine spread. It looks like Martha Stewart vandalized my personal space.

Adding to the weirdness, a T-shirt has been laid out across the foot of my bed. I edge closer, taking in the shirt's full horror. It's baby pink with a white fuzzy kitten on the front. The kitten's collar is studded with glittery pink rhinestones and it stares up at me with wide blue eyes. Is that glitter dusting the kitten's fur? Holy crap, it is.

"Hi, sweetie," a voice says behind me. I whirl around, almost falling onto the bed.

Mom stands with one hand braced against my doorframe, smiling tentatively. Her hair is in a loose bun, renegade strands clinging to her neck. She's wearing her old robe, ratty and blue, with one pocket sewn on sideways in red thread. Claire and I learned to sew when I was eight by practicing on that robe. I'd like to point out that Claire is the one who sewed the top of the pocket closed. I'm just responsible for the red thread. I picked it out after

31

Claire pricked her finger with the needle and bled all over the blue thread we initially chose.

Mom hasn't worn that robe since Claire died. I thought she threw it out with the garbage and her motherly instincts. My stomach twists looking at our lopsided stitches. I want to both hug Claire and jab her with the needle a few more times. But that's the thing about dead sisters: can't do much with them.

"Hi?" It comes out as a whisper.

"Do you like it?" Mom asks, gesturing toward my bed.

Ah. Apparently Mom is responsible for that monstrosity. I thought Emmet was screwing with me, but guess not.

"It's—uh—very pink." The words are so pathetically stupid I cringe. My mother is standing here. In my room. Talking to me. For the first time in forever I can yell and scream at her, let her know just how pissed off I am about being left a virtual orphan, and she might actually hear me. Except I can't. Because my mother is standing here. My mother. I'm afraid to move in case she retreats back into her fog and forgets me again.

"You like it, right?" Mom moves past me to lift the T-shirt up. She smiles and runs a finger across the rhinestones. "You've always loved kittens and pink's your favorite color."

My favorite color is dark blue. Mom knew that once.

"Yeah, it's great," I choke out. If I were Pinocchio my nose would be knocking a hole in the wall.

"I'm so glad you like it," Mom gushes. She sets the T-shirt back on my bed and fusses with the sleeves. "I saw it at the store and couldn't resist buying it for you. You look so pretty in bright colors. I talked with my supervisor about switching my schedule around and I'm going to start working the day shift on Saturdays. Maybe the three of us can have the occasional dinner together again. Will you let Emmet know?" She turns back toward me, hands fluttering at her side.

"That'd be great," I say slowly, holding my breath. Any minute, a TV camera crew is going to jump out of my closet and shout "Surprise!" Or I'll wake up, alarm blaring.

Instead, Mom gives me an unsteady smile. Her fingers brush the sideways pocket and her smile disappears, eyes unfocused and glassy with the beginnings of tears. "I'm sure you've got plans for the evening so I'll get out of your hair."

"No, I—"

She pats my shoulder vaguely and drifts out of the room.

I retrieve my camera and snap a picture of the hideous T-shirt; yet another photo for my wall. Even when Mom sees me, she's not really seeing *me*. I tack the picture beside a self-portrait I took a few months ago. In the image, half my face is obscured by the bulky camera and the rest of me is dark and blurry, a distorted reflection in my bathroom mirror. I am just a shadow girl these days.

CHAPTER FIVE

Anarchists for Cheesus

It takes me a while to pull myself together after Mom's little visit, but I manage to make it to work on time. Andy is grinning when I arrive at the Gas & Gut. I have Monday nights off so this is the first time I've seen him since he found Baby Cheesus. He stands behind the main counter, an open pack of potato chips beside him, playing an exaggerated drum solo in the air with battered-looking chopsticks.

"Guess whose blog got a million hits today?" Andy says, smacking an invisible cymbal and then gesturing for me to answer with one of the chopsticks.

"Oprah?" I ask.

"Please. I kicked her touchy-feely, let's-hug-the-world ass."

Andy drops the chopsticks, pulls out his iPhone, and flicks it on before thrusting it into my hand. A blog page fills the screen, garish in crimson and black with the anarchy symbol anchoring the top. Below the masthead, a picture of Baby Cheesus takes up most of the page.

I smirk. "Love the blog theme."

Andy jabs a finger at the blog's hit counter. "That's more traffic than this entire town has seen in the last century. I'm famous."

He has a point, but I'm not going to stroke his ego. His blog's sudden popularity is nothing but morbid curiosity.

"I thought you sold the cheese wheel?" I hand the phone back.

Andy frowns. "Yeah. Wish I hadn't, but it was Uncle Bobby. What was I supposed to do? He said Baby Cheesus belonged with the church and God would reward my charity and piousness. He also started hinting that he expects me back at services. He can be scary intense."

Andy hasn't been to a service in over a year. His dad is drunk most weekends, and his mom died when he was three. Bobby helped raise Andy, but two years ago Andy declared he was an atheist and pissed off every white-hair in town. Bobby's been trying to bring Andy back into the church ever since. So far, he hasn't managed it.

"You're scared of Pastor Bobby? How's that fit with your whole drugs, anarchy, and rock 'n' roll philosophy?" I laugh as Andy pulls my apron from under the counter and throws it at me.

"You've heard him preach about hell. That man means business." Andy widens his eyes and fakes a shiver.

"Pastor Bobby has a set of wind chimes on his front porch made out of beer cans and wears a bass fishing shirt every day but Sunday." I shake my head. "Not scary. At all."

Andy shrugs. "You weren't standing here with him staring you down. At least I was the first to post a picture of Baby Cheesus. I found the thing, that counts for something."

"Sure. Like finding a crispy fried pinkie finger in your French fries at Burger King. It's an honor." I finish tying my apron on and give Andy my best crazy smile.

"You're just pissed you didn't find Baby Cheesus," he says.

"Please, I am totally fine with your newfound fame."

Andy lifts an eyebrow but waves me behind the counter. "Don't expect to find another miracle cheese, I already checked."

I glance at the dairy case. The green mesh basket that normally holds the Babybel cheese wheels is empty again. "I hope you paid for those or Ken's gonna fire you. Famous or not."

"Settle down, I paid for them. Not a single religious symbol anywhere." He waves a hand, giving me a rueful smile.

"Guess God is done playing with food."

"You want help counting out your cash drawer?" Andy waggles his eyebrows like he's suggesting something dirty.

"No, thanks, I can handle the big scary numbers."

Andy smiles and hooks his thumbs into his belt loops. "You're missing out on prime Andy time." He heads for the front door, calling over his shoulder, "One million hits, Del. One million!"

I laugh and wave my hands, shooing him away.

On Wednesday, the Ballard County Times runs a paragraph about Pastor Bobby purchasing Baby Cheesus. It's on page three, but it's still there. On Thursday a late-night TV show host mentions the miracle cheese during his opening monologue. Andy's blog is up to three million hits and Baby Cheesus has gone viral, pictures popping up on Twitter and Facebook.

Friday morning, I shoulder my backpack and shove my way through the crowd at school. The rows of yellow lockers stretch out ahead of me and my sneakers squeak against the dingy linoleum floor. Gabe is already at his locker, spinning the dial and smacking the metal door when it sticks.

Wendy and Anna stand a few feet away, close enough that I can hear them without any effort. They look like they coordinated their outfits, each wearing a pink baby doll tee and white jeans. It's gagworthy.

All is not well in clonesville, however. Anna's hands are on her hips and one foot taps impatiently. Wendy's crossed arms are definitely giving off a defensive vibe. Trouble with the super-friends?

"You promised," Anna whines.

Wendy grimaces. "I can't. Daddy says it's sacrilegious to take Baby Cheesus on house calls. He's built a special pedestal in the church and a plexiglass box to hold Baby Cheesus."

Anna scowls, foot tapping faster. "But you took it to Trish's house and she got an A on her chemistry test. I'm failing algebra and my hair is a disaster. You promised Baby Cheesus could help."

"I would bring Baby Cheesus over if I could!"

Anna sags back against her locker, shoulders slumping. I grab my books and stop next to Gabe.

"Did you hear that?" I ask in a low voice, nodding toward the two girls. "Bobby's displaying Baby Cheesus in the church?"

Gabe rolls his eyes. "Dad's been ranting all week about it." He slams his locker door shut and glares at the lock. "He keeps muttering about false prophets. He's obsessed. Cheesus is all anyone wants to talk about."

37

"Wanna talk dramatic plot devices instead?" I gesture at *Twelfth Night* and Gabe's grip tightens on the book, scrunching the cover.

"I can't focus. It's all prithee this and prithee that. Who talks like that? I can't understand half the words."

"That's why it's great literature. If everyone could understand it, it wouldn't be great."

Gabe shakes his head. "My mom had a thing for Shakespeare. She used to read me *Much Ado About Nothing* when I was in kindergarten. I should get this stuff by like genetic predisposition or something."

"Guess you skipped those genes. But, hey, you got a full dose of nerd genes so it's not a total loss." I let the quip about his mom pass. It's dangerous territory and Gabe's already in a bad mood. Lila Beaudean hasn't been in touch since the day she left Clemency six years ago. Every couple of months the two of us try Googling her name but so far, nothing.

"Shut up," Gabe mutters, a smile tugging at the corner of his lips. All the same, I can tell he's still thinking about his mom. Nothing else makes his eyes go so blank.

Time for a strategic topic change. I tap the toe of his shoe with mine. "The stuff with Baby Cheesus will blow over. Anyway, shouldn't you be the first one in line praising the miracle cheese?"

Gabe straightens and narrows his eyes. "Because I'm a preacher's son?"

"I thought you'd be into religious signs and all that." I tug Gabe's arm, herding him toward homeroom. "Your dad too."

The tension drops out of his shoulders and he sighs. "Not when the religious sign in question is sitting in

St. Andrew's and Pastor Bobby is gloating about how he's got a divine object and Dad doesn't."

"So you don't think there's anything to Baby Cheesus? No chance it's real?" I'm not sure which way I want him to answer. Gabe's always had enough faith for the both of us, and this past year, faith is something I've been a little short on.

"I haven't even seen the thing. All I know is it's driving Dad nuts, and he's driving me nuts. I need the cycle to end."

We reach homeroom and I give Gabe a mischievous smile. "Maybe God will send your dad a divine French fry or something."

"Not funny. Let's drop it, okay? I really am tired of hearing about Baby Cheesus." Gabe flops into his seat with a scowl.

All through class, my brain keeps circling back to the question of whether that cheese wheel is real or not. I mean, I know it's real; I saw it. I touched it. But what it means is a whole different problem. I'm kind of erring on the side of "It's all bullshit," but there's a tiny part of me that's got questions. I attended church every Sunday growing up, took communion, said my prayers each night like a good little girl. I believed, one hundred percent, that God was watching over me and my family. Right up until Claire got sick. When my sister died, that was pretty much it for me and God. Clearly he didn't have my back, why should I have his? But it's hard to let go of something you've believed your whole life.

Chapter Six

Dinner Derailed

Saturday night, I'm standing outside the bathroom Emmet and I share and kicking the door.

"Come on, Emmet! I need to pee, get out of there."

"Hang on!" he growls back. The door stays locked. I huff out a breath and lean my forehead against the wall. Emmet's been monopolizing the bathroom for the past twenty minutes, and it's starting to get annoying. If I was truly desperate, I'd brave Mom's room and the master bathroom.

Finally the door opens and I straighten, take in the full picture of my brother, and burst out laughing. "What did you do to your hair?"

"Shut up." Emmet's voice is sullen and he shuffles past me, glaring.

His hair is sculpted into a wave and he's pulled little strands loose to flop over his forehead. An emo football player. I should snap a picture and send it to *Ripley's Believe It or Not*.

"So," I draw the word out, flicking a finger at his snazzy bangs.

Emmet swats my hand away.

"Who's the girl?" I ask

Emmet turns red. Interesting. "You don't know her," he mutters.

I narrow my eyes. Has he resorted to picking up city girls? How? Rust Bucket would cough out a radiator if he tried to drive the thirty miles to Ashby.

"Impossible," I say.

Emmet stops blushing and glowers at me. "Suddenly you're the social queen? You and Gabe spend your time talking about nerd stuff and ignoring the world. I bet you wouldn't recognize half the freshman class."

My mouth drops open. "You're dating a freshman! Who? Carly Harmon?" She's cute and she spent most of the summer making puppy dog eyes at Emmet.

"I said you don't know her. I met her at an away game last season and we've been texting for a while."

"Wow." I give him a sly look. "How do you work the phone keys with those gorilla hands of yours?"

Emmet tries to swat me again but I duck into the bathroom and slam the door in his face, locking it.

"Better hurry," I croon sweetly through the door, "don't want to be late for your date." I sing-song "date," drawing it out. Emmet thumps the wall and stomps off.

If Emmet's got a hot date, I guess I'm on my own for dinner. Leftovers, here I come. I'm ten feet from the kitchen when my nose registers the smell of tomato sauce and spices. I approach the kitchen as though it's a bear trap, unwilling to discover those wonderful scents are my imagination working overtime. Mom is standing by the stove, stirring something in a big silver pot.

Emmet sits at the table, fingers flying over his phone.

"Hi, sweetie," Mom says in a cheerful voice, turning to smile at me. "You're just in time. The spaghetti sauce has another ten minutes before it's ready. Be a dear and grab that colander from the sink. The noodles need to be drained."

41

I don't move. "What's going on?"

Mom's smile becomes strained at the edges. "We're having dinner. I told you I switched my Saturday shifts."

Oh. Right. I didn't think she was serious. And because I didn't think she was serious, I never bothered to tell Emmet about Mom's dinner plans. Which explains the narrow-eyed look he shoots me before focusing on his phone again. Oops.

Emmet finishes whatever he's doing with his phone and tosses it onto the table. "I told Micah we'll hang out tomorrow after services."

Mom nods and snatches another pot off the stovetop. "Del, the colander?"

My feet drag in slow motion to the sink but I make it there in time to hold the colander up while Mom dumps in the noodles. One of them slops over the side and wraps around my wrist, a soggy, wet tether.

Mom laughs and plucks the noodle away. "Thanks. Emmet, can you get out plates? Del, why don't you start the garlic bread."

She's acting like all of this is totally normal. Like I haven't been living off Beefaroni and day-old pizza for ages. As though the past year hasn't happened at all. Make that two years because that's how long it's been since we had pasta night as a family. I glance at the colander. The pile of noodles reaches to the top of the bowl. Way too much for three people. But then, Mom's used to cooking for five.

"Del, what's wrong with you tonight? Can you please help with the garlic bread?" Mom's voice snaps my attention back to her and I drop the colander into the sink, noodles and all, and move to the fridge. My body's on autopilot. I should call bullshit on all of this, but the spaghetti sauce simmering on the stove smells amazing and Mom's smiling. Sometimes it's just easier to go along with things. I'm not forgiving her, just calling a temporary cease-fire.

Ten minutes later the table is set, the sauce is ready, and I'm placing a slice of garlic bread beside each plate. Mom beams at Emmet, me, the table, as though we've performed an amazing circus trick and she might start clapping at any moment. It's a little creepy.

Between slurping noodles, Mom grills Emmet about his new girlfriend. "How'd the two of you meet? How long have you been dating? What's her name?"

I expect Emmet to answer with a grunt, as usual. He holds in words like a dragon hoarding treasure when it comes to talking about the girls he dates. Instead, cheeks red, he smiles and says, "I met Micah at a football game six months ago. She was—uh—there with the other team."

"Are you seeing anyone, Del?" Mom asks.

The dream about kissing Gabe pops into my head, and I choke on a mouthful of garlic bread. Emmet starts laughing.

"No," I manage to wheeze out.

Mom looks concerned but I wave a hand at her and snatch up my soda bottle, downing a few gulps.

The phone rings and Mom gets up, preempting Emmet. She checks the caller ID and frowns. "Why would Maybelle be calling at this hour?"

Maybelle Jensen is the biggest busybody in town. If she's calling it's nothing good.

Mom answers with a too-bright "Maybelle!"

Emmet snorts and shovels in another mouthful of food.

Mom's quiet for a long time, listening, before finally saying, "I see. Of course we'll try to be there." Pause. "Yes,

43

that does sound amazing." A longer pause. "I have to go, Maybelle. The kids and I are in the middle of dinner. We'll catch up tomorrow."

Mom's cheerful tone has cracks in it the size of the Grand Canyon and her face is pale. The phone shakes in her hand as she gingerly sets it back in the stand.

"What was that about?" I ask.

Mom drops bonelessly into her chair and stares at the tabletop. "There's a special service at St. Andrew's tomorrow. Pastor Bobby has asked everyone to do their best to be there."

"Which service?" Emmet frowns. The football team always attends church together during the late morning service. Coach says it builds team cohesion and Emmet's always moaning about having to drag his ass out of bed in time, but he'd never miss a Sunday. Rumor is, Coach benches anyone who isn't a regular church attendee.

"The eight thirty service," Mom answers, still distracted.

"What's the big deal?" I ask. Mom's acting weird. She attends the first service at St. Andrew's every week anyway, so that can't be what's bugging her.

She lifts her head and meets my eyes, frowning. "Do either of you know something about a holy cheese wheel?"

I laugh in relief. "Is that all? Yeah, everyone's talking about it. Andy found it at the Gas & Gut a week ago and Pastor Bobby bought the thing."

"Maybelle said it's a genuine miracle, that it can heal the sick," Mom whispers.

I go still. That's the same tone of voice Mom used the day my parents told us Claire had cancer. As though the words are coated with shards of glass.

"But it's not real." My voice is higher than I want and I clear my throat, suck in a deep breath. "I know Wendy Stevenson's claiming she was healed, but looked at the source! Remember that time she told everyone a spaceship made crop circles in Mr. Hadley's field? Only it was just his cow rampaging around after a fence blew down?"

"Maybelle says there have been several healings." Mom stares at the table, smoothing her hand over the paper towel beside her plate. "Can you imagine if Claire . . ."

She trails off and Emmet gets up, coming to stand behind her. He rests a hand on her shoulder. "It's okay. She's okay now. She's with God."

I shoot him a dirty look. He's always bought into that whole "it's all okay because she's in heaven" crap. Claire was thirteen. She should be here with us.

Mom looks up and there are tears sliding down her cheeks, but she smiles at Emmet. "You're right, of course." She pats his hand and gets up. "I'm just being silly. I think I'll go lie down for a little bit."

Emmet mumbles a reply and Mom stumbles past him. Her hip knocks into the table, sending her dinner bowl smashing to the ground. Pasta sauce splatters across my shins, staining my jeans, but Mom doesn't pause. She walks out of the room completely oblivious, back in her haze.

I might as well be invisible.

CHAPTER SEVEN

Cheesus on the Pulpit

I slink out of the house an hour early the next morning. Considering how badly things ended last night, I want to be out the door long before Mom and Emmet start moving. It's too early for my shift at the Gas & Gut, but I head there anyway. The store is quiet, right up until church lets out. The handful of cars that pass through town on the highway don't stop.

Around noon, a steady stream of people begins filtering through the store. Each and every one of them wants to buy a cheese wheel. We run out within half an hour.

A little after one, Gabe stomps into the store. He's still in his dress shirt and slacks from church, his mouth a grim slash. He looks good in dress clothes. I try not to notice the way his shirt is just a bit too tight in the shoulders, but it's a losing battle.

"How'd you get out of youth group?" I ask, fumbling for something to say.

Gabe frowns, forehead scrunching. Did he catch me checking out his shoulders? I want to sink behind the counter and hide. There's a long, awkward pause. Finally, Gabe grabs a large cup and fills it with ice and Dr. Pepper. He takes a sip before passing me a dollar. "Pastor Bobby lured half our congregation away this morning. Dad's furious. I slipped out and he didn't even notice."

I stop willing myself to disappear. "Pastor Bobby put the word out last night that he wanted everyone at a special service today. Something about Baby Cheesus."

"Yeah." Gabe rests an elbow on the counter and sighs. "Bobby's got that thing on display in St. Andrew's chapel, right beside the pulpit. Only way you get to see it is by attending services."

I give him a sideways look. "You went to St. Andrew's?"

He flushes and laughs. "I slipped in after the late service ended. If Pastor Bobby wasn't so long-winded I wouldn't have had time. The cheese wheel really does look like a baby in swaddling cloths. There was a huge crowd looking at it, and not all of them were townies."

The bell over the front door rings, and another person wanders in asking to buy a cheese wheel. Gabe waits, but more customers arrive. Eventually he gives up, shoots me a wave, and says we'll chat later.

My shift ends at three because I picked up some extra hours earlier in the week. I grab my backpack and dash out the door, barely saying a word to Andy.

St. Andrew's sits at the southeast corner of town, three blocks from my house. My feet keep moving past my front door and on toward the church. I pause at the stop sign and take it in. The tall white spire stretches high over a set of thick wooden doors. Stained glass windows stand in even rows down the side walls, colorful bursts amid the white paint. On the front lawn at least thirty people mill around, chatting in small groups. Some of them are sitting, legs tucked beneath them, leaning close and whispering. Wendy Stevenson and several of the blonde brigade sit near the front steps.

Before anyone notices me, I take my camera out and get a picture of the crowd in their Sunday best, the church

47

framed behind them. I'll label it WORSHIPING A DIFFERENT GOD. How many of them came to hear Pastor Bobby preach and how many came just to see the cheese wheel?

As if I'm any different. It's not religious fervor dragging me back to St. Andrew's, but simple curiosity. I take a deep breath and brave the crowd.

Wendy must have some sixth sense because her head whips up when I'm a few feet away and she breaks into a huge smile. "Welcome back! You're a little late for services."

I gesture at the people gathered on the lawn. "What's going on?"

"Impromptu prayer circle. We thought it'd be nice to sit out here and soak in some sunshine while we pray. People kept getting distracted in the sanctuary."

I glance at the front doors.

"Here to see Baby Cheesus?" Wendy asks.

I nod slowly, shifting my backpack on my shoulder. Yeah, I've already seen the cheese wheel, but I want a second look. Just hearing about it sent Mom scurrying back to her room last night. What did she see this morning when she looked at Baby Cheesus?

Wendy grimaces and gives a little shrug. "Daddy says it can only be displayed during services, so that we're showing the proper devotion. Baby Cheesus isn't a circus sideshow. Sorry. I'm sure he'll bring it out next Sunday if you want to come back. You're welcome to join us for prayer circle, there's always room for one more."

Wendy pats the grass next to her with one hand and gestures at Anna with the other, urging her to make room. Anna frowns but moves over a few inches. I'd have to be skinny as a stick bug to fit into that space.

"Nah," I say, backing up a step. "I've got chores to do at home. I was just curious, no big deal."

"I hope we see you next week," Wendy says, offering another encouraging smile.

Not likely.

That evening, I have dinner at Gabe's house. I'm here at least once a week so it's a comfortable routine. His dad is late, and when the front door creaks open, we're already in the kitchen, staring into the mostly empty refrigerator.

Gabe pokes a carton of eggs. "We could have breakfast for dinner."

"How old are those?"

He shrugs. "I don't think they're going to hatch if that's what you're worried about."

"What are you two up to?" Mr. Beaudean asks, coming into the room.

I look over my shoulder and offer a tentative smile. His tie is loose, suit jacket already off. He's handsome for an old guy, with a round, friendly face and permanent laugh lines. Normally, he moves like there are springs coiled beneath his feet, but now his steps drag and there are dark circles under his eyes.

Gabe shuts the refrigerator and turns toward his dad. "Sizing up dinner prospects. It's kind of bleak."

"How about we order a pizza? Think I've got a coupon around here somewhere."

Gabe grins. "Can you get extra pepperoni and sausage on half?"

"Don't I always?" Mr. Beaudean heads for the phone, pausing to squeeze Gabe's shoulder. It's just a casual gesture, the sort of thing parents do all the time. The sort of thing my parents used to do all the time. I clear my throat because it's suddenly too tight to breathe.

At the dinner table half an hour later, I lift a large slice of greasy pizza and slide it onto my plate. Maggio's Pizza is the closest shop, and one of the few places that will deliver in Clemency. It's New York–style pizza with huge slices, thin crust, and enough cheese and toppings that you could scrape them off and make an extra meal. Pure heaven.

Gabe groans appreciatively as he takes a bite. Some cheese catches on his bottom lip and I resist the urge to lean over and wipe it off with a finger.

Mr. Beaudean dabs at the top of his pizza with a napkin, sopping up the grease. He's changed into an Oklahoma University T-shirt, the short sleeves frayed at the ends. Normally, Gabe's dad chats about church stuff and interrogates us about our week. Tonight he's quiet and spends most of dinner frowning at his pizza. It creates a weird tension in the room. In the background the *drip, drip* of the faucet punctuates the awkwardness.

Gabe glances over his shoulder at the sink. "We should get that fixed. Want me to call Mr. Hollis?"

Mr. Beaudean looks up. "I'll take care of it later."

"Seriously? Last time you picked up a wrench you dropped it on your foot."

"It's a leaky faucet, I'm not calling in a handyman for that."

"You called Mr. Hollis this summer when the bathroom drain was blocked. And last year when the living room fan went into turbo mode and wouldn't switch off."

Mr. Beaudean gets up from the table, his pizza missing only two bites. "We need to fix that roof leak at Holy Cross. Money's tight for everyone right now and tithes are down. Any spare money I can scrape together needs to go back into the church. I'll take care of the sink."

Gabe stops protesting and his dad leaves the room, shoulders slumped.

"Shouldn't the church council be the ones taking care of the roof leak?" I ask.

"Yeah. But like Dad said, tithes are down and there isn't enough in the church budget." Gabe lowers his voice, looking at the kitchen entrance. "He's been donating half his paycheck back to the church. He doesn't know I found out, but he left his checkbook lying out the other day. We had to cut our elder care meal service down to twice a week last month and Dad's taking it pretty hard."

"I didn't know things were so bad." I put a hand on Gabe's arm and he gives me a reassuring smile.

"It'll turn out all right. Dad's always said God provides whatever we need, we just have to be patient. Although it's been a while since we've had to be this patient."

He gets up from the table and dumps his empty plate in the trash, then yanks hard on the faucet handle. The spout continues to drip.

"Want help cleaning the church tonight?" I ask. I may avoid the services, but I usually help Gabe with cleanup duty on Sunday nights. It's part of our routine.

"Yeah, let's get out of here."

The sun is just dipping past the trees and the world is purple gray. Sunset is my favorite time of day because it's like the world is watching me with sleepy eyes, everything mellow and calm.

Holy Cross used to be a bank. The front is all heavy stone arches framing a set of truly obnoxious wood doors. There's a statue of a cross out front to clue anyone passing by into the building's status change.

Gabe unlocks the church door and we step inside, flicking on the lights. After the church purchased the building, the interior was gutted and a wall built to divide the worship area from the lobby where they serve coffee and doughnuts each Sunday morning from the front desk. I can already see a coffee cup stashed behind one of the potted plants and a service program lying by the women's bathroom door.

"Ten bucks says I find more coffee cups than you do," I say.

Gabe grins. "You're on."

We race off, Gabe breaking left, me right. It's amazing how many people abandon their cups, or deliberately hide them, before heading into morning services.

Fifteen minutes later I have five cups to Gabe's four. A third of our usual haul.

"Count them and weep," I crow, shoving the cups into Gabe's hands. I already dumped the leftover coffee into the water fountain from the two cups that were half full. No way I'm sloshing coffee all over the floor, even in the interests of winning. I don't do mop duty.

"Did you plant these?" Gabe narrows his eyes at me.

"I was working? Remember?"

"I suppose. But I don't entirely trust you, Delgado."

"I'm wounded, Beaudean."

I spin on my heel and sashay into the main worship area. "Come on, slow poke, lots to do still."

In the far corner, past the pulpit, the ugly water stain that appeared on the white ceiling tiles a few months ago is bigger. Reverend Beaudean is right, they'll have to take care of that before the next big storm hits. Fall in Texas always brings a monsoon or two.

Gabe and I walk down each pew row, straightening Bibles in their chair back holders and picking up crumpled programs. It doesn't take long. I like Holy Cross at night, when it's just Gabe and me. There's a different kind of quiet in here that feels comfortable. The frenetic energy from the day is gone.

"Dad seemed better tonight, don't you think?" Gabe asks when we're done.

"Than what?"

"I think he's finally dealing with the Baby Cheesus situation. Maybe we won't have to dance around the subject anymore."

"You really want to talk about it with him?"

"No, but it's better than not talking about it with him, you know? Like it's taboo, so it's always there."

We lock up the church and swing back by Gabe's house to grab a cup of coffee before I head home. It helps me unwind at the end of the day and Gabe's taken up my bad habits.

As soon as we hit the front porch, we can hear his dad yelling somewhere inside the house.

"Don't tell me that wasn't underhanded!"

Gabe eases the door open and we tiptoe inside, stopping in the entry hall. His dad must be on the phone in the kitchen.

"You're luring people into St. Andrew's under false pretenses to see that stupid cheese wheel," Mr. Beaudean snarls.

There's a pause, then, "I damn well will call it what it is. I'm all for friendly competition each week, Bobby, but this is a new low."

Pause.

53

"You know exactly what I'm accusing you of. If you want to tout that thing as a holy relic I can't stop you, but stop displaying it during services. You may as well be running a side show."

Gabe and I share a guilty glance. How mad will his dad be if he catches us eavesdropping? But neither one of us moves.

"You want to come over here and say that to my face? Tricking people into attending your service is unchristian."

After another long pause, Mr. Beaudean's voice gets even louder. "First it's name-calling and now you're going to start insulting my church? We're not five-year-olds. And don't you dare imply that a grocery store reject gives your church some sort of holy seal of approval."

Mr. Beaudean slams the phone down and Gabe and I jump at the sound. We bolt for Gabe's room, shutting the door behind us as quietly as possible.

Gabe shakes his head and drops onto his bed. "I take it back. Dad isn't handling Baby Cheesus well at all."

Chapter Eight

Not Exactly a Picasso

That week things are pretty tame. There's lots of talk about Baby Cheesus, and even the kindergarteners have seen Andy's picture of the cheese wheel. But there are no more miraculous cures, not according to Wendy anyway. Mom's back to skulking in her room and heading out for her night shift early. Business as usual.

Pastor Bobby has the cheese wheel on lockdown and rumor is it won't be back in its plastic case in the church until Sunday. Where he's keeping it in the meantime is anyone's guess.

Saturday night, Emmet and I wait at the dinner table for half an hour before finally giving up and going our separate ways. Mom never even pokes her head out of her room, and when Emmet knocks on the door she tells him she's too tired to cook.

Sunday comes and goes. The attendance at Holy Cross is still down. Gabe's dad is still upset and Pastor Bobby has switched the sign outside St. Andrew's to read HOME OF THE HOLY CHEESE. I snapped a picture. My Cheesus-related snapshot collection is growing steadily.

Tuesday, when I go on shift after school, Ken is standing by the door with an impatient frown. Not a good sign. I dart a glance at the clock hanging on the back wall, but I'm five minutes early.

Ken is paunchy and short, with a ring of hair clinging above his ears like the fat friar in a Robin Hood movie. He always wears Hawaiian shirts, even in the middle of winter. Today's shirt is orange with green parrots and salt-crusted margarita glasses printed on it. If there's ever a natural disaster in town, we could use that shirt as an emergency beacon.

Ken nods at me as I step around the counter and tuck my backpack onto a low shelf. "We need to discuss the front window."

I dart a look at Santa and then back at Ken. How'd he find out about my plans to add a cowboy hat to Santa's ensemble? I haven't done it yet, but I've got the paints stashed in my bag.

"You got a decent hand with a brush," Ken says. "I saw that ribbon you got at the art show. I think it's time we replace the window display with something more timely."

"Sure," I say, eager now. I'll get to paint and I won't have to worry about Ken freaking out over his window display being ruined.

"I want it to say 'Cheesus Was Here' in big red and yellow letters, and below that a picture of Baby Cheesus. Can you manage that?"

My shoulders droop and I sigh. I wasn't expecting to recreate a Picasso, but still.

"Yeah, I can do that."

"Great!" Ken pulls a folded paper from his back pocket and smooths it out to show a grainy picture of Baby Cheesus. "I should sack Andy for selling that cheese wheel to Bobby. It was found in our store, it shoulda stayed in our store. That boy's brain is full of holes. But we can still get some mileage outta the cheese. I ordered two cases of Babybels for this week, and with this in the window, we might need to go to four cases."

"When do you want me to start?" I try not to sound as disgusted as I feel.

"Now. I bought some paints and brushes. They're in the back. You let me know if you need extras. You can paint between customers."

"Am I getting a bonus for this or something?"

Ken laughs and pats my shoulder. "You're on the clock and besides, you did say you'd do whatever was needed around the store if I let you clerk."

"I figured." I shrug it off and go looking for the paints. Good-bye, Santa; hello, Cheesus. It's just trading one fictional character for another.

Chapter Nine

Jesus and a Side of Fries

There are a lot of things you miss out on when you live in a small town: malls, big concerts, endless shopping and dining opportunities, comic book shops, and casual crime. Fast food, however, is one of the few universal institutions across America.

On the way to school Thursday morning, Emmet and I notice a dozen cars filling the McDonald's parking lot and a small crowd of people surrounding the drive-through window. There's no such thing as fast food rush hour in Clemency, at any time of day, let alone breakfast.

Emmet is so distracted, Rust Bucket's front wheel hits the curb and he overcorrects, swerving wildly before getting the car under control.

"What the hell! Cars go on the road, not the sidewalk." I rub my right shoulder, tender from slamming into the door panel.

Emmet ignores me and mumbles, "Someone must've been murdered."

He pulls into the McDonald's parking lot and parks sideways, blocking a line of three cars. There are trained monkeys that can drive better than my brother. We get out and join the crowd. I recognize a couple kids from school, and most of the adults, but there are a few new faces—people passing through town on their way to Houston or Dallas, or maybe religious nuts here to see Baby Cheesus. Despite the Sunday-only viewing schedule, a few people show up each day trying to get a peek at the miracle cheese wheel.

Ahead of me, the drive-through window is blocked by the jostling crowd, and I stand on tiptoe trying to see.

"Is it real?" someone asks from the front of the crowd.

"It looks genuine." That sounds like Bill Henderson, the McDonald's manager. "Jim said it was on the window when he opened the store this morning. He called me right away."

I jab Emmet in the ribs a bit harder than necessary. "What is it? Can you see?"

Emmet shakes his head and shoves forward, aiming for the out-of-towners. They won't be around later, and any fallout from trampling them will likely be minimal. Occasionally, my brother is smart. We shimmy and elbow our way to the front of the crowd.

The drive-through window has some sort of whitish stuff obscuring the glass.

Emmet sucks in a breath. "Holy shit."

Mr. Henderson's head snaps around and he gives Emmet a narrow-eyed look. "That sort of language is uncalled for, especially under the circumstances."

I duck around Emmet and come up on his other side, trying to get a better view.

"Holy shit." I stare at the window.

"Del!" Mr. Henderson snaps.

"Sorry," I mutter.

The white stuff is semi-opaque; I can see the dim out-line of the grills and cash register through it. But more importantly, the white forms a negative image: a guy's face with a beard and long hair. It looks uncomfortably like that famous shroud thing, the one that Jesus was supposedly wrapped in. The Shroud of Touring or something. Even I know what that looks like.

"Is that—" My voice trails away.

Emmet nods. "Jesus."

Mr. Henderson darts a glance at Emmet but evidently decides he isn't cursing this time. "Looks like Jesus to me."

"How is that even possible?" I ask.

"It's a miracle. Another miracle," someone behind me says. Cell phones are held aloft and the *whirr-click* of pictures being snapped underscores the growing whispers. Beside me, a lady in a pink jumpsuit bumps my arm as she tries to get a better angle with her camera phone.

I edge closer to the window. "What is that stuff?"

Mr. Henderson shrugs. "No idea. Seems like the image has been oxidized into the window pane."

The word miracle gains force like a wildfire, jumping from person to person. The whispered conversations and exclamations are getting louder too.

The pink-suited woman bursts into tears and I turn to look at her, only then realizing she's my second grade teacher, Mrs. Keller. Her phone is pink as well, with little jewels on the case, and she's staring at the picture on her screen, sobs catching in her throat. "God is with us!"

I purse my lips. "It's on a drive-through window. That's hardly divine."

"Ain't nothing wrong with our food," Mr. Henderson says in a loud voice. "Even God approves of a good meal."

"It's probably someone playing a joke." I raise my voice, gesturing to the window. "Someone could have painted that thing."

Someone gasps, and I turn to face the crowd of people. Most of them are glowering at me and a few look ready to burn me at the stake. One of the out-of-towners, a large man with a fanny pack bisecting his beer gut, is nodding, however.

"Girl's right," fanny pack man says. "This is probably a publicity stunt or some advertising thing."

Mr. Henderson clears his throat. "I can assure you this is not a marketing campaign. That image is real. Just look at it."

"You shouldn't question God, Delaney," Mrs. Keller says. She's done crying but her face is blotchy and red. "It's blasphemous."

"Everyone knows that girl's turned her back on the Lord," someone calls from the back of the crowd. Is that Maybelle? I can't tell, but it sounds like her. Old bat.

Emmet stands behind me and puts a hand on my shoulder. "Del doesn't mean any harm, let her be."

I jerk my head up and stare at him. He's glaring at the crowd with an I-dare-you-to-say-something look. Why would he defend me? Most days we barely talk. My chest squeezes tight and I have the sudden urge to hug my brother.

"Now, folks, let's keep things under control," Mr. Henderson says. "This here miracle is plain as can be. God himself is showing his approval of our town. First that cheese wheel and now this. We are blessed."

The crowd nods and for once I keep my mouth shut.

Mrs. Keller drops to her knees and starts praying. "Lord, thank you for blessing us with your presence. Thank you for the miracles you work every day and for reminding us to look for them."

Several others kneel, and Mr. Henderson crosses himself.

"People'll believe anything," fanny pack man says, making a dismissive noise. He grabs the arm of a thin woman standing beside him, her summer dress bright pink and blue, and begins backing out of the crowd. The woman glances wistfully over her shoulder at the window, but allows herself to be pulled away.

Carla Murphy, a cashier at the McDonald's with hair black as asphalt and acne scars on both cheeks, jostles to the front of the crowd, taking advantage of the gap left by fanny pack man and the woman. She reaches her hand out to touch the glass but Mr. Henderson catches her arm and shakes his head.

"Don't want to get fingerprints on Jesus, now do we, Carla. Where's Jim? Have him bring out the tool set and we'll take down the window."

The crowd grumbles. "You ought to leave that where it is!"

"I've got a business to run, don't I?" Mr. Henderson says. "People want their hotcakes and fries."

Emmet squeezes my shoulder and says in a low voice, "Let's get out of here."

I nod and start toward the car. The people in front of us move to the side, pressing forward to fill the tiny gap we leave. I get several narrow-eyed looks.

Back in Rust Bucket, I take a deep breath and turn to Emmet. "Thanks."

He grimaces and stares straight ahead, refusing to look at me. "You're my sister. It's not like I could stand there and let them rip you apart."

Rust Bucket starts up with a wheezing cough and we pull out of the lot.

"You got that vibe from them, too, huh?"

"You're good at pissing people off."

"Gee, thanks for the pep talk."

"You know what I mean. You should go to services and keep your head down. People in this town don't like anyone who's too different. If you just go along it'll make life easier." Emmet hesitates. "What have you got against St. Andrew's, anyway? Mom'd be happy to have you go with her."

Yeah, I'll just bet she would. She'd probably forget and drive off without me.

"I don't have anything against St. Andrew's," I snap. "I just don't feel like going to church anymore."

"You used to go all the time." Emmet's using his calm, reasonable voice. I want to slap him.

"I used to believe there was a point. Or didn't you notice Claire's gone? All that praying didn't do anything."

"Don't use Claire as an excuse for your hang-ups," Emmet growls.

"They're not *my hang-ups*. It's simple logic. Way I see it, there are three options." I count them off on my fingers with insulting slowness. "God doesn't exist, God does exist but he can't do a damn thing, or God does exist and he killed Claire. Personally, I'm liking option number one. Either way, I don't see the point in wasting my Sunday mornings."

Emmet rolls his eyes. "We might have just seen proof that God exists. Would it kill you to admit miracles are possible?"

"We never got one. If miracles are real and God has time to go around finger painting on drive-throughs, then why the hell couldn't he help Claire get better? Why couldn't he keep Dad from running out on us, or Mom from turning into a living ghost? If miracles are real, where were ours?" I make a disgusted noise. "We saw a windowpane with a blurry image. That doesn't mean God was strolling around town. When did you become so gullible?"

"When did you stop believing in anything?"

The words punch me in the gut and tears gather at the corner of my eyes. Before I can think too hard about why I'm about to start crying, I slam out of Rust Bucket and storm toward the school.

Chapter Ten

Doubting Del

Gabe is waiting on the school steps. He glances between me and Emmet and then grimaces. "Family drama?"

"Yeah. Emmet's willing to believe anything and of course I'm a bitch for not buying into it too."

Gabe follows me as I storm inside.

I stop in front of my locker and try to melt the tiny lock with my eyes. I feel like a geyser on the edge of blowing, fury and hurt bubbling under my skin. How dare Emmet talk to me like that, try to guilt me into going back to St. Andrew's. I went to church after Claire died. All the nice old ladies gathered round and patted my shoulder and talked about God's will. As though that made everything okay. They're just words. They can't bring my sister back, fix my family, or change the things I said to Claire before she died. My mind skitters away from that last thought, shoving it back in the dark hole where it belongs before guilt chokes me.

"What aren't we buying?" Gabe asks.

I turn and lean my back against the locker, dropping my bag at my feet. Some of the anger leeches away, but my voice is still bitter when I answer. "God left a calling card on the McDonald's drive-through window. Apparently I'm the only one who thinks a divine message at Mickey

D's is weird." Gabe's eyes are wide, but he waits for me to finish. "Emmet's pissed I'm not ready to jump on the holy sign bandwagon. He says I don't believe in anything."

Gabe hesitates a moment too long. Great, just freaking great. He agrees with Emmet, doesn't he?

"You've never been shy about your feelings," Gabe says tentatively. "Not about God or church or any of it."

And there it is. The mountain we've been ignoring for the past year. The preacher's son and the newborn atheist. How can our friendship possibly work, let alone anything else between us?

"You never talk about God when I'm around," I accuse. Maybe Gabe doesn't bother spouting gospel at me because he's not sure there's anything in me worth saving. The thought hurts more than Emmet's words in the car.

Gabe shifts, fingers worrying at the ends of his backpack strap. "It's not like I talked about God all the time before . . ." His voice trails off.

"Claire. You *can* say her name, you know."

"You were so angry when she died. I didn't know what to say. And then you stopped going to church and snapped at anyone who even mentioned God in passing. I didn't want to hurt you more or shove my beliefs on you. If you want to talk God, I'm ready to listen or share or whatever. But just because I believe in Him, it doesn't mean you have to as well for us to be friends."

"Doesn't it?" My voice is half pleading, half angry. The warning bell rings, but I ignore it, eyes locked on Gabe. Around us, the other kids hurry to class, clutching books and shooting us sideways looks.

"No. We're friends for a hundred different reasons. Because you punched Wayne in the face when we were kids. Because we used to camp out in the backyard. Because I helped you steal Mrs. Henderson's underwear off the wash line and put it on Maybelle's fat old basset hound. Because being friends doesn't mean you have to be the same. Because you'd stand between me and a grizzly bear if it came to it. And I'd do the same for you. We promised to always be there for each other."

"We were ten when we said that."

"I don't break my promises."

Mr. Rayburn, our history teacher, marches down the hall, herding a trio of boys ahead of him. "Gabe, Del, warning bell already rang. Get to class."

Gabe and I share a quick glance, tabling the conversation for now. I grab up my bag and we fall into step with the guys: Kevin Pierce, Wayne Hissep, and Neil Clover—all jocks and members of the unofficial boys' smoking club. I'll bet Mr. Rayburn caught them sneaking a cigarette in the parking lot.

Gabe nudges my arm as we approach homeroom. "I want to hear all about the holy drive-through. It's embarrassing being the last one to know. I'm supposed to have connections! The way Wendy tells it, I should be on God's speed dial."

I'm still feeling shaky but I appreciate the peace offering. "Okay. But if we get caught passing notes, you're explaining my detention to Ken."

Despite Gabe's burning need to know about the McDonald's incident, we don't actually pass notes in homeroom. Neither of us is that crazy. Mrs. Winnacker has evil superpowers and can sense a note being passed from fifty feet away.

I should work on my algebra homework, but I can't concentrate. Two religious signs this close together can't

67

be a coincidence. Someone must be faking them. I flip to a fresh page in one of my notebooks and begin jotting down a few names: Pastor Bobby, Andy, Wendy, Mr. Henderson, Ken. Each of them had opportunity and any one of them could be behind the whole thing. I'm not sure why they'd be faking miracles or how I'll prove which of them is doing it, but a suspect list is a good place to start. I can figure out motive later.

My phone, a little Nokia with a postage stamp screen, vibrates in my pocket, distracting me. With Mrs. Winnacker glowering at us, I don't dare check it. Later, in the hallway, I flip open my phone and an image pops up—a blurry picture of the McDonald's drive-through window. The message is from Wendy with the caption "Another miracle!" and a smiley face.

I may need to move Wendy higher on the list.

I hold my phone out for Gabe to see. "Clemency's latest miracle, courtesy of Wendy."

During lunch, Carly Harmon joins us at our table. She's had a crush on Emmet forever and occasionally she chats with me in an effort to get closer to him. Her tactics are way off. My brother doesn't consult me for dating advice. As far as I can tell, if it has two legs, a cheerleading outfit, and a high-pitched giggle, Emmet will date it.

Carly's not on the cheer squad and thus out of luck. Today she's wearing a sparkly silver tank top and super-tight jeans. I think her outfit's supposed to make her look older but it's more like she raided Hooker Barbie's closet.

"Did you hear about McJesus?" Carly asks, breathless.

Gabe grins at her. "McJesus? That was quick. Took them at least a day to come up with a name for Baby Cheesus."

Carly pouts. "You already know."

"Yeah, Del saw it this morning."

Carly's eyes widen and she gives me her full attention. "Was it really the face of God? I heard it appeared in a ray of light and that people who saw it knelt down and started praying. A real live miracle. Not a factory defect like some people are saying about Cheesus."

"I didn't see a magic ray of light. It was just a splotchy white image." I scowl down at my chicken nuggets.

Carly's enthusiasm dims and she leans close to Gabe, her shoulder brushing his. "What do you think?"

I narrow my eyes. Is she making a play for Gabe? Maybe she finally got the memo that Emmet's not interested. I dig my nails into my palms so I don't shove Carly off her seat. Gabe can do much, much better.

"I'm going by after school," Gabe says, oblivious to Carly's sudden interest. "Sounds like it's worth a look at least."

"I'd love to—" Carly begins, but Wendy sweeps up to our table with Trish and Anna trailing behind her and Carly falls silent. Just in time. I'm certain she was going to ask Gabe to take her with him. One more word and I'd have been forced to start a food fight with Carly. The cafeteria chicken nuggets are hard enough to qualify as lethal weapons.

"I heard you saw the miracle this morning," Wendy says, smiling at me.

I stare accusingly at Gabe. "Did you tell everyone?"

"Not me!" He holds up his hands, playing innocent.

69

"Emmet told Kevin the two of you stopped at McDonald's before school," Wendy says.

Ah. My big-mouthed brother. Well, it's not like this is a state secret. I sigh. "Yeah, we saw it. I was just telling Carly."

Wendy bounces in place. "I told you there were miracles happening!" Her voice is gleeful. I guess she's not pissed her daddy doesn't have a monopoly on so-called holy relics anymore. Unless he buys the window from Mr. Henderson. Maybe that's his master plan and he's planting miracles so they can't be directly linked to him. Then he just buys them afterward. Wendy continues, "I want to know everything! Brandy Park was there and she says her twisted ankle was healed. What did it feel like standing next to a divine image?"

"Crowded," I mutter, still distracted by my new theory.

Wendy frowns. "Don't be flip. This is serious. There's a sort of energy when you stand next to Baby Cheesus, this amazing feeling of calm and peace. Was the window the same way?"

"I honestly didn't notice."

"What *did* you notice?" Anna demands in a snide voice.

"A lot of camera phones. A lot of people. Window with some white stuff on it. It wasn't very divine if you ask me. I mean, why would God be hanging out at McDonald's? It's not exactly last supper material."

Wendy huffs out a breath. "You were front and center at a miracle. You'd think it would've made more of an impression."

It's making an impression now. Wendy could be orchestrating this whole thing. She's been pushing the idea that Cheesus is a miracle from day one. And she was the first to report a miraculous healing, even if it was utterly ridiculous. Plus her dad is benefiting from Baby Cheesus, winning the church wars for the first time in forever. Wendy is such a daddy's girl, I bet she'd think faking the miracles to help out St. Andrew's is just being a good daughter.

"Del's not easily impressed," Anna says.

"I don't believe every story I'm told," I agree.

"But you saw it—" Wendy starts.

Gabe cuts in. "Anyone have a clear picture of the window? The only one I've seen was small and blurry." Nice distraction. Full points to Gabe.

Wendy fishes an iPhone out of her purse, taps it a few times, and then holds it out to Gabe. "Brandy took that this morning."

Carly and I lean forward, peering at the phone as well. The white image on the glass is hard to make out. In person, the image resembled a face. On Wendy's phone, it looks more like a dancing bear.

"Isn't it exciting?" Wendy burbles. She returns the phone to her bag and beams at us.

I'm definitely moving her to the top of my suspect list.

CHAPTER ELEVEN

Easy as ABC

Emmet peels out of the parking lot the moment I slide into Rust Bucket after school. I scramble to pull on my seat belt and sigh. The Delgado civil war continues; guess he hasn't forgiven me for this morning's argument.

Rust Bucket slows as we pass the McDonald's.

Outside, a news crew is setting up. One man balances a camera on his shoulder, while an older guy with a beer gut to rival Ken's is busy checking a clipboard. Ten feet away, a pretty redhead fusses with her hair and checks her makeup in a tiny compact. She's dressed in a blue suit with a pencil skirt that definitely didn't come from the local Walmart. The three of them look as out of place as a herd of cows in the school gymnasium.

A white van with the ABC logo splashed across the side sits near the restaurant's front doors. I guess the red curb with NO PARKING painted on it doesn't apply to reporters.

"Wanna check it out?" I ask.

Emmet makes a snorting noise under his breath, but pulls into the lot. A news van in Clemency qualifies as free entertainment. We park and get out without a word.

Claire was our peacemaker, navigating the fights and arguments over the years and negotiating terms of surrender. Without her, our arguments can stretch on for weeks. I wonder how long this one will go?

Other cars are pulling into the lot as well. Inside the restaurant, a few patrons stare at the news crew, their food forgotten. There's already a handful of people forming a semicircle on the sidewalk. Emmet and I join them.

"Lucy," clipboard man calls, glancing impatiently at the redhead and motioning her over.

She frowns but puts away her compact and takes a few steps closer. "Ready to shoot?"

Clipboard man shakes his head and checks his phone. "Margie hasn't been able to reach the preacher. I want shots of the other supposed miracle as well."

"I can get pickup footage here," the cameraman says, "and we can interview some of the locals. That will take time."

Clipboard man nods. "Okay. Set up inside. Manager has the window behind the counter on a stand. We'll shoot an intro next to the register."

The news crew heads inside, and like marionettes pulled on strings, the crowd follows behind them, Emmet and I shuffling along as well.

A minute later the redhead beams and tosses her hair back as she looks into the camera. "This is Lucy Ralston, reporting from tiny Clemency, Texas. Residents were startled this morning to find what some are claiming is the face of Jesus on a drive-through window at McDonald's. Two weeks ago another religious image, the figure of baby Jesus, was spotted on a cheese wheel from a local convenience store. Is God at work in this little town? Many residents believe so."

There's a pause and then clipboard man says, "That's good, Luce. Let's run it through one more time, I want to hear that smile in every word. Jim, make sure you get a good shot and as Lucy's winding up, zoom in on the window. I want a clear picture of the face. Shooting again in 5 . . . 4 . . . 3 . . ." Clipboard man falls silent, holds up two fingers, then one, and finally points at Lucy.

Lucy runs through her speech again. And then again. Meanwhile, more people join the crowd behind us, trying to see what's going on. A short while later, the TV crew starts interviewing Mr. Henderson.

While Lucy Ralston smirks and Mr. Henderson extols the virtues of fast food and divinity, clipboard man gets on his phone again. His frown deepens as he listens and barks out short one-word answers. When he puts the phone away, he looks as though someone put pepper in his coffee.

"The preacher's secretary said he's filling in for the chaplain at Central Point Hospital in Petersville. She won't let us see the cheese wheel without him there."

"Are you talking about my daddy?" Wendy's chipper voice breaks in from behind me. I twist around to find the blonde brigade and a dozen other kids from school pressing close. Just visible at the back of the new scrum of people, I can see Gabe's curly brown-blond hair.

Wendy elbows her way forward, not even noticing me as she shoves past. She stops in front of clipboard man. "You were talking about Pastor Stevenson, right?"

Clipboard man nods slowly, and then breaks into an ingratiating grin. "Any chance you can get us in to see the miracle cheese?"

Wendy pulls out her phone and makes a show of finding her dad's number. "Of course," she purrs. She pauses a moment with the phone pressed to her ear. "Daddy? Yeah, everything's fine. There's a news crew asking to see Baby Cheesus. Can I take them over to the sanctuary?" Another pause. Wendy's face falls. "But I'll be right there." She wheedles for a while longer before tucking the phone back into her purse with a sigh. "Daddy says he'll be back at five. If you want to wait, he'll take you to see Baby Cheesus then."

Clipboard man glances at his watch and scowls.

Lucy Ralston taps a foot and glares at him. "I have dinner plans, and they don't include the local chicken shack."

Clipboard man straightens and glares back at her. "We can run some more interviews with locals and shoot intro shots around town. Let me call Bob and make sure he's fine with the delay."

Lucy throws her hands in the air. "It's a two-minute segment, Carl. We have enough footage, don't we, Jim?" She turns to the camera guy but he shrugs, refusing to commit.

"This could be picked up by the main network," Carl says. "It's the sort of human interest piece they like to run. Might even make it onto the CNN homepage. If we need it, I want the additional footage. Those bastards at CBS aren't scooping me again."

Lucy tilts her head, eyes widening. "You think it could go national?"

Carl nods. "Human interest," he repeats.

Lucy fusses with her hair again and straightens her perfect skirt. "Who do we interview first?"

Wendy takes a tiny step forward. "I can tell you all about Baby Cheesus."

She launches into a description of the cheese wheel and how her *dear* cousin Andy first found Baby Cheesus. Blah, blah, blah. But a moment later, Wendy says, "And not only has Baby Cheesus brought our congregation

75

together, it's also brought my cousin back to the church, which is a whole other miracle in itself."

My eyebrows shoot up. Since when is Andy attending services? It's not like we braid each other's hair and swap secrets, but Andy and I chat between shift changes. Wouldn't he have mentioned being roped into St. Andrew's again?

Lucy wraps up her interview with Wendy and her eyes land on me. I drop my scowl, but not quickly enough. "We should get an opposing viewpoint. What about that young lady?" Lucy points a red fingernail at me and my heart drops.

Wendy laughs nervously. "Del's shy. She doesn't want to be on TV."

Suddenly, Del wants very much to be on TV. Nobody gets to speak for me, especially not Wendy. "I'd love to be interviewed."

Lucy beams. I swallow hard and hope I'm not making a huge mistake. We deal with the formalities first, my name, age. Then Lucy launches into her questions with a look in her eye that's disturbingly similar to a piranha being tossed a steak dinner.

"What do you make of this sudden miracle mania, Del? Do you think God is sending a message to your town?"

"I think it's a load of crap." There's an audible gasp in the crowd. "I mean, seriously? Two miracles so close together? That's fishy. Plus, what's with the food thing? If God was going to send us a message, wouldn't there be a burning bush or something?"

"How do you explain the cheese wheel and this latest appearance?" Lucy asks. She's trying to be earnest but can't hide the glee in her voice. She wants drama and I'm delivering in spades.

The camera guy pans away from my face and sweeps the crowd, recording their reactions. I take a quick glance as well. There are a lot of glares aimed my way. I might need a police escort out of here and possibly a stint in the witness relocation program. But I've already pissed everyone off so I might as well keep going.

"I think someone's faking them."

Another gasp from the crowd, louder this time.

"That's a serious accusation," Lucy says.

I shrug. "It's the best explanation."

Wendy can't contain herself anymore, she shoves forward, stopping beside me. "Del's just joking. Of course the miracles are genuine. Anyone can see that. There have been several spontaneous healings. I personally got over a very serious illness after praying beside Baby Cheesus."

Lucy quirks her eyebrows and Wendy babbles on, stepping in front of me. While the news crew is distracted, Emmet grabs my arm and drags me several feet away. People part to let us pass like I'm coated in skunk spray, all wrinkled noses and pained expressions.

"Are you crazy?" Emmet demands. "What were you thinking saying that stuff to a reporter?"

"I was thinking someone needs to start using their brain around here and asking a few questions." I yank my arm free and glare at my brother. "It's a free country, I can say what I want."

Emmet growls under his breath. "You are dumb as a rock if you believe that. All you've done is make a lot of people mad. The whole town is going to turn against you if you keep acting like this."

"Let them," I snarl. Before he can lecture me anymore I shove past him and lose myself in the crowd. A couple people try to stop me, reaching out as if to grab my arm, but I brush past, keeping my head down.

I run headlong into someone and reel back. Strong hands catch me before I can fall.

"Hey, easy," Gabe says.

I stop struggling and melt against his chest. "Please tell me you brought the Taurus."

"Let's get out of here."

The Taurus actually belongs to Gabe's dad, but Reverend Beaudean lets Gabe drive it whenever he wants. Thank goodness he has the car today. He pops the locks and I dive inside. My backpack is still inside Rust Bucket, but I can grab it later. We're quiet for several long minutes while Gabe maneuvers out of the parking lot. The tension gets thicker with every second.

"That was pretty intense," Gabe says, finally.

"Yeah."

"Not sure that was the smartest move, though."

"Not you too!" I snap, swiveling in my seat to face Gabe. Unbelievable. "So, what, I'm just supposed to bow down at the altar of the holy cheese? Just go along with everyone else because that's the easy thing to do? Pretty sure we watched a video about this in middle school. It's called peer pressure and it's a bad thing."

"Whoa, don't bite my head off."

"I've already listened to one lecture from my brother, I don't need one from you." The car stops at a red light and before Gabe has a chance to say anything else, I fling my door open and get out. "I can walk. Thanks for the ride."

The door slams on Gabe's response and I storm off. I glance back once and Gabe is still sitting there, even though the light has turned green. He's staring after me with his mouth slightly open, hands slack on the steering wheel. As if I'm the one talking stupid and not him. *Not the smartest move.* Where does he get off? I can't be the only one who thinks there's something weird about these miracles. I figured analytical super-nerd Gabe would at least consider the possibility.

Gabe's supposed to have my back no matter what, not side with Emmet. Everyone is turning on me, the town, my brother, and now my best friend. A dozen times today, I thought about sharing my suspect list with Gabe. I'm glad I didn't.

Chapter Twelve

Saint Claire

Just before dinnertime, Mom emerges from her room and stumbles downstairs in her Everything Store vest. She hasn't bothered to put her hair up and her eyes are puffy and red-rimmed. There's a tissue clutched in her hand and she keeps tearing off little pieces with her fingers, dropping them like confetti on the floor.

She pauses on the last stair and I watch her warily from the kitchen doorway.

"Hi, sweetie," Mom murmurs. Her voice sounds water-logged and hoarse.

"Did something happen? Is Dad okay?" I demand, a surge of fear squeezing my throat.

"What?" Mom's eyebrows lower and she shakes her head. "No, everything's fine. I haven't heard anything from your father so I'm sure he's all right."

"Okay." I draw the word out, slow as a bad Wi-Fi con-nection. Her shirt is buttoned up wrong and only tucked in on one side. She's wearing one navy sock and one black sock. My mother, even in the midst of Claire's many med-ical crises, has never looked anything less than put together and calm. Yeah, she's a virtual stranger these days and does her best to avoid Emmet and me like we've got the plague, but she's never been a slob. The woman standing in front of me now is an utter mess. Clearly something is wrong, even if she's not willing to say what it is.

Oh no. Does she have cancer too? Emmet? These things can be genetic, right?

"You could tell me if something was wrong, you know," I say, trying to pretend panic isn't dancing a hula in my stomach.

"I'm just being silly," Mom says with an unconvincing laugh. "Maybelle called again, about the McDonald's drive-through. I keep thinking, if only this had all happened last year, maybe it would have made a difference. Maybe the miracles would have helped Claire."

"That's why you're crying? Because you think some painting on a window could've fixed Claire?" My voice shakes.

"That cheese wheel and the window are miracles, Del. Of course they could have helped her. They just came too late." Mom wrings her hands together, looking ready to cry again.

"They're both fakes. They have to be," I snap.

Mom gives me a sympathetic smile, hands twisting together. "I know you're hurting, honey. I understand. But turning your back on God isn't the answer."

"He turned his back on us first," I fire back.

Just then the front door opens and Emmet strolls in. He makes it two steps into the entryway before stopping and looking between Mom and me. "What's going on?"

Mom ignores the question, eyes locked on mine, face bewildered. "Why are you acting like this?"

"I'm not acting like anything."

"What'd you do now?" Emmet accuses, frowning at me. Of course he'd immediately take Mom's side, even when he doesn't know what side that is. She's ignored him for months, but let her give him a scrap of attention and he'll heel like a good little boy. No, thank you. I have more pride than that. All her talk about us being a family again, about Saturday night dinners and spending time together, such crap. Look how quickly that fell apart.

"I didn't do anything except point out the obvious," I snarl at Emmet. "God didn't send that cheese wheel or the McDonald's window. Don't you get it? He doesn't care. He's not tossing out miracles like candy. It's all a stupid hoax and I'm the only one who sees it."

Emmet groans. "Are you still going on about that?"

Fury at Emmet and my mom has tears scalding my cheeks, but I shove them away with the back of my hand.

Mom looks tiny and sad. "You girls were so different. Your sister always believed with her whole heart and you always questioned everything." Mom gives a hiccupping laugh. "I couldn't drag you to church now if I had twenty horses and a strong length of rope. But Claire never missed a service; even in the hospital she always asked for the chaplain on Sundays."

"That's bullshit." The words drop like bombs between the two of us. Emmet moves toward me but I back away from him, still focused on Mom. "You don't even know who Claire is anymore. Maybe you never did. Stop pretending she was this perfect angel."

"Del!" Mom's face is crumpling in on itself, a black hole of grief and pain, but I can't stop.

"The real Claire was a whiny brat who stole my dolls and drew on their faces." Emmet tries to interrupt but I give him a dark look and barrel on. "She hated having cancer and being sick. She was pissed at the world. She was pissed at God."

"Stop it," Emmet whispers. His eyes are so wide, pleading with me.

All the words I've been holding inside come crashing out.

"You act like you owned Claire, Mom. Like you're the only one who's allowed to miss her. She was my sister. And she wasn't perfect—she didn't have to be. It's like you think her life isn't worth anything if she wasn't this amazing person. You know what?" I spit the words like scorpions, stingers raised. "Claire was ordinary. Not beautiful. She was a lousy singer. She had no fashion sense. She drew on the walls and had smelly socks. She wasn't the one calling the chaplain in every hour in those last weeks, that was you. I am so tired of the myth of Saint Claire. It's like having her die all over again listening to you make up stories about her. I can love Claire without her being perfect. Why can't you?"

Tears stream down Mom's face, and Emmet rushes to her side, pulling her into a hug.

"How can you say those things about your sister, Del? Why are you doing this?" Mom sobs.

Emmet squeezes Mom tighter and looks at me like I'm pond scum. "Happy?"

"Everything I said is true, whether you want to hear it or not." My words fall flat with only the ghost of defiance left in them. But I don't regret anything I said. I don't. I bolt past Emmet and Mom, heading for my room.

At my dresser, I pause and stare at my reflection. My eyes are too bright, my cheeks flushed apple red. I will never be my mother's perfect, dutiful little girl. I can't compete with Claire's ghost.

Claire's death wasn't graceful and neither was she. She raged and screamed and kicked. She was a bitch and furious with the world for stealing her life. She was real. And in the end, she wasn't singing songs and telling the world she loved them. She probably left this Earth flipping it off.

I don't know. I wasn't there.

I was at home because there had been two weeks of last nights. How was I supposed to know this really was the last one? That I'd never have a chance to take back the things I said the last time I sat beside my sister?

I say she was flipping the world off, but that's how I want to picture her. In the end, Claire was in a coma, just a body occupying space. All that rage and temper and life drained away and left a shell behind. One night she stopped breathing and left me for good.

Right up until the end, my parents were convinced that one more prayer session would fix everything. Even now, all Mom can think about is how everything would be different if these so-called miracles had shown up early. As if Baby Cheesus and that drive-through window are anything more than a stupid prank taken way too seriously by our nutso town.

Emmet, that ass-kissing traitor, hates having to go to church every Sunday with the team, no matter what he tells Mom. At least I'm honest about not knowing what to believe any more.

I kick the side of my dresser. Pain shoots up my leg and it feels good. Real. I kick the dresser again and again.

"Del!" Emmet stands in my doorway, glaring at me. "What the hell?"

"Don't act like you care." I flop back onto my bed. My foot throbs in time with my heartbeat, too fast.

"Why are you acting like a psycho?" Emmet braces a hand against the door, still standing in the hall. He hasn't been in my room since Mom moved Claire's stuff out.

"Why aren't you backing me up and telling Mom those miracles are fake? Because maybe you didn't notice, but it sure looks like crazy town from where I'm sitting. I mean, Jesus at the drive-through? Come on!"

"Maybe the miracles are God's way of showing us Claire is okay, that she's with Him." Emmet sounds as lost as Mom and it just makes me angrier.

"She's dead and everyone still acts like she's the center of the universe. Not everything is about Claire. Some jerk is faking miracles, probably because he thinks it's funny. End of story." I roll over and press my face into my pillow, smothering a scream.

"Stop throwing tantrums just because nobody buys your ridiculous conspiracy theory. Grow up, Del."

I sit up so quickly my head spins and I fling my pillow at Emmet. He dodges it and sneers, "You're hurting Mom by acting like a crazy bitch. Get it together." Emmet doesn't wait for my response, just slams the door behind him. The walls shudder with the force of it and I expect my door to come crashing in, all dramatic. But it remains in the frame. I want to hurl my dresser at the wall and smash everything to pieces, have a real tantrum like Emmet accused.

Instead, I lie back on the bed and stare at the ceiling, thinking about the miracles and how much they're screwing up my life.

CHAPTER THIRTEEN

Just Like Scooby

There's a knock on our front door later that night, close to nine o'clock. Mom left for her shift hours ago, and I heard Emmet leave shortly after—probably off drinking at a stupid pasture party with his friends. I'm still pissed over the fight earlier but my urge to kick the furniture has faded.

I open the door to find Gabe fidgeting on the doorstep.

"Hey," he says. He looks ready to dive for cover. Can he see the signs of the fight with Mom reflected in my face?

"Hey." I back up a step and Gabe smiles tentatively, coming inside.

"Wasn't sure you'd let me in." He hunches his shoulders and I stare at him for a moment before remembering I left him sitting in the middle of the road at a stoplight. It feels like a week ago instead of a few short hours. After everything with Mom and Emmet, Gabe's comments in the car seem trivial.

"Of course I'd let you in." I should apologize for running off but the words are stuck in my throat. I shuffle into the living room and flop down on the couch instead. Gabe follows and when he sits there's an entire couch cushion and a world of unsaid words between us. The awkward silence grows until all the air is being sucked out of the room.

"I'm sorry," we both begin and then break off with nervous laughs.

"I didn't mean to flip out earlier," I say. "I just can't understand why no one else is questioning this stuff. I mean, I know why you're going along with it. You're a preacher's kid so of course you have to believe in miracles. I shouldn't get mad at you for something you can't help."

"Gee, thanks." Sarcasm coats his words like a fine dusting of powder.

"I'm trying to make up," I mutter.

"Your technique seriously sucks. I don't believe in the miracles because my dad's a preacher. I believe in them because I believe in God. Because I know there are things in life that can't be explained. Admitting the miracles might be real isn't a crime."

"So you think God's endorsing McDonald's?" I try to keep my voice neutral but it borders on sarcastic.

"I don't think God's giving fast food his stamp of approval. But that window has everyone's attention. If I was going to leave a religious message, I'd want maximum impact."

"Why not make it appear at the church? I mean that's where all the believers are."

"Yeah, so that's the last place you'd put it. This way even people who don't go to church see, and maybe it gets them thinking."

"Or buying more French fries."

Gabe sighs. "Every time I suggest anything you either shoot it down or launch into a snark attack. I'm not going to just nod my head and agree with everything you say, Del. We're allowed to have different opinions."

I open my mouth to respond, but shut it just as quickly. My default answer these days is almost always sarcasm.

"I'm sorry. I wish I could believe as easily as you do. But nothing makes sense anymore, least of all this."

Gabe nods. "I know you've had it rough since Claire. But just talk with me, okay? Truce?"

His voice is so tired and I can feel the same weight pressing down on me. "Truce. But I can't get on the miracle bandwagon. I just can't."

"No one's asking you to. But it's a big leap from not believing in the miracles to announcing they're fake on TV. They could both be natural phenomena. There doesn't have to be some mastermind behind it."

"If it was just Cheesus or the drive-through window, maybe. But the two of them so close together? That can't be coincidence."

"Which brings us back to the miracle theory."

"And the jerk with a warped sense of humor theory."

Gabe nods reluctantly. "I guess it's a possibility as well. But they're just theories. There's no proof either way."

"We could find some. We could prove, definitively, that the miracles are fake. Or that they're real," I add quickly, catching Gabe's annoyed expression.

"And how are *we* supposed to do that?" There's a subtle emphasis to his words that twists my stomach into a knot.

"I've started a suspect list," I admit, watching Gabe closely.

His eyes widen the tiniest bit and he blows out a breath. "Who's on it?"

Before I can change my mind, I get up, grab the notebook from my backpack, and flop back onto the couch beside Gabe. "Are you sure you want to hear this?"

"Might as well, you're going to keep looking into it whether I'm helping or not. And you know what they say: two nerds are better than one."

The old joke, the one we use to yell at my brother when he teased us for trying to build bottle rockets in the backyard, makes the muscles in my shoulders relax the tiniest bit. Gabe's here and he's listening. I take a deep breath and rattle off my list.

"What are their motives?" Gabe quirks an eyebrow.

"Motives?" I repeat, like it's one of Mr. Sutherland's fiendish math problems.

"Don't you watch *Sherlock*? Detectiving 101: there's always a motive," Gabe adds.

"Bobby's winning the church wars for the first time in forever and having a fun time doing it. Wendy's a daddy's girl so anything that benefits her dad makes Wendy happy too. Ken would sell his left kidney to bring in more customers and put the Exxon out of business. Andy . . . well, I'm not sure. Extreme boredom?"

"Mrs. Deardly?"

I flush, knowing she's the least likely of all my suspects, but I felt like the list needed a bit of padding. "She's a creepy old lady. And suspicious. You know she buys the same thing every time she comes to the Gas & Gut? A bottle of cough syrup and a pack of peppermint gum. She wears dentures, so she can't even chew gum!"

"McJesus wasn't painted with cough syrup or sculpted from chewing gum, so I'm not getting the connection. Acting weird doesn't mean you're a criminal. If it did, half this town would be locked up."

"There's a difference between quirky and weird. Quirky is okay. Quirky is Jim Wilco's belt buckle collection. Weird is a little old lady who's never had so much as a sniffle buying cases of cough syrup." I pause, struck by a horrible thought. "Maybe she's running a meth lab, like *Breaking Bad*. But with old people."

Gabe snorts. "That's your craziest theory yet. And *how* does that give her a motive for faking the miracles?"

"New customer base from all the out-of-towners? Distract the local police?"

"You need to watch less TV. Or at least better TV."

"Shut up. You wanted motives, it's not my fault you don't like them."

Gabe reaches over and grabs the notebook, yanking it free. He begins flipping through the pages. "I'm playing devil's advocate. If you go accusing anyone of faking the miracles, you better have a ton of proof."

"So you admit it's a possibility?" This is more important than it should be. If I can convince Gabe, then maybe I can convince other people as well.

He sighs. "Maybe. But what happens if you start poking into things and you find out the miracles are real? What are you going to do then?"

I shrug. "I'll deal with it." Easy words. But I'm not going to have to deal with anything because there is no way those miracles are real.

"Fine. I'll help you investigate. What do you want to do first?"

My chest burns and I suck in a deep, shuddering breath. "Really?"

"Really. But if we find out they're real, we share that info as well." His face is stern. He looks so much like his dad in that moment, every bit the preacher's kid.

I lean over and hug him, squeezing as tight as I can. My notebook is smushed between us and the spiral coil digs into my skin even through the material of my shirt.

"Okay." I pull back a little and we're so close our breath tangles together. The tension from earlier morphs into a different kind of tension and I get up from the couch before I do something stupid, like kissing Gabe. My notebook falls, forgotten, into Gabe's lap and I can't quite meet his eyes.

"It'll be okay," Gabe says. "We'll figure things out and everything will get back to normal soon."

I'm not sure if he means the town, our friendship, or something else. I shrug off the awkward feelings and paste on a smile. "Let's talk motive."

Chapter Fourteen

Good Morning, Clemency

The ABC news piece on McJesus runs during the ten o'clock news, right after a segment on a bungee-jumping Chihuahua. Gabe sticks around long enough to watch, trying and failing to hide a wince when my interview is aired in its entirety. Afterward he gives me a quick hug and then heads home. The next morning, there's another article in the Ballard County Times about McJesus. I scan the words as I shovel down some Froot Loops. According to the article, Mrs. Abernathy, one of the school board members, is claiming McJesus healed her laryngitis, and Reggie Groom, the guy who owns Groom's Hardware, says his bum knee is suddenly fine.

Gabe is waiting for me by the school doors as usual.

"You see the paper this morning?" I ask, my voice too loud.

Gabe nods. "Yeah. Guess Reggie won't be limping around the store today. But miraculous healings kinda point to, you know, a real miracle."

"Placebo effect," I scoff. "Like when the doctor gives you a sugar pill, but you think it's medicine so you get better anyway. There was a show on Discovery Channel about that last year. Claire and I watched it at the hospital." I don't add that Claire laughed her butt off and said maybe she'd be better off if her doctors switched her chemo to sugar water. I brought her a glass of water and five sugar packets each day for a week after that; she mixed them with methodical care and drank every one. Sometimes, Claire and I were good together in that last year. It's easy to forget with everything that came after.

"I guess," Gabe says. But I can tell he wants to believe the healings are real. "Dad talked with Mr. Henderson yesterday, asked if we could hang McJesus in the church on Sunday. But Mr. Henderson said he wasn't moving McJesus anywhere—the restaurant has been packed since the news van yesterday."

"Your dad chewed Pastor Bobby out for putting Baby Cheesus on display. Why's he want McJesus?"

Gabe shrugs. "Attendance is way down."

"A splotchy drive-through window isn't going to solve that."

"Works for Bobby." Which is a good point.

We walk into the school and at first, everything's fine. But then the comments and looks start.

"Nice interview, Del," someone calls. The words have jagged edges, meant to draw blood.

I whip my head around, trying to find the speaker, but I'm met with a hallway full of glaring people. Judging by the numbers, half the student body would like to kick my ass right now. It was just a stupid interview for goodness sake.

Gabe moves closer to me, so that our shoulders brush. "Just ignore them, keep going," he mutters under his breath. We keep our heads up and shuffle to our lockers. By the time we get there, the muscles in my shoulders are so tight you could bounce quarters off them.

Wendy swishes down the hall toward us. Her hair is done up in a twisty braid and she's wearing extra makeup, smiling like she won homecoming queen. The other kids move out of her way without being asked. While I'm being treated like something nasty found rotting on the side of the road, Wendy has ascended to celebrity status.

Wendy stops in front of me, her smile turning kind and extra sweet. I can feel a diabetic coma coming on in response.

"Del," she coos. "Last night's interview was just a bitty mistake. I'm sure you didn't mean any of the things you said. That reporter swooped in and surprised you! Not everyone reacts well to the spotlight."

Wendy preens, obviously replaying her time in front of the camera in her mind, and I am utterly speechless. But not for long. "I meant every word." I keep my voice low and lethal.

"Del!" Wendy sounds genuinely shocked, like I've shoved a knife into her gut. "You've stood in the presence of God's holy gift to this town. You saw the image of Jesus on that window. Now I know you've struggled a bit with last year's unfortunate events, but there is no reason to spit in God's face."

"Last year's unfortunate events?" I repeat, shaking with fury. "My sister died. A thirteen-year-old kid. Was that the Lord's loving hand at work? His mercy?" Gabe puts a hand on my shoulder but I shrug it off and get right in Wendy's face. I'm so close I can see every pore beneath her makeup, every blemish and imperfection. "Miracles don't happen. That cheese wheel and the window are a joke."

Tears fill Wendy's eyes and her voice is husky. "It's just pain making you say such awful things."

I want to wipe that look of pity and understanding off Wendy's face permanently. Gabe must sense the violence

94

rising up in my gut because he grabs my shoulders and yanks me back against his chest, fingers digging deep into my skin so I can't jerk away.

"Del's just fine. She's got a right to her opinion," Gabe says, making Wendy frown.

"She hasn't been to church in months," Wendy counters. "She's risking her soul by speaking out against God the way she did yesterday."

"I said the miracles are fake. Get your facts straight," I snap.

Wendy shakes her head slowly. "That's as good as speaking against God. He sent the miracles."

The warning bell rings, ending Wendy's lecture. She sighs and pats my arm. "I'll keep praying for you." Then she walks off, head high and shoulders back.

I sag against Gabe. I wish he'd let me hit her, but it's probably better he didn't. I wasn't suspended for any of my fights last fall, but I suspect things might be a bit different today.

"We should get to class," Gabe says, close to my ear.

I shiver and nod.

In history class, I discover why Wendy's dressed like a presidential hopeful and looking so smug. The ABC segment was rebroadcast on *Good Morning America*. Mr. Rayburn recorded the segment and plays it for us on the pretext this qualifies as current events. The whole segment lasts maybe three minutes and he switches it off after Wendy's interview, just as my face appears on screen. Mr. Rayburn glowers at me for a moment before getting himself under control and turning to beam at the class.

"This is the first time Clemency has been in the national news!"

A couple of boys in the back of the room high-five. I keep my back straight and ignore the sideways looks I'm still getting. After the confrontation with Wendy this morning, no one's had the stones to say anything directly to me, but there are a lot of conversations that end mid-word as I pass by. Gabe goes out of his way to walk with me in the halls, even though it makes him late to class a couple of times. By the end of last period, I'm not sure if I want to cry or punch something. Things haven't been this weird since the first weeks after Claire died, when everyone treated me like a bomb that might explode at any second.

After school, Gabe and I don't make it farther than the McDonald's parking lot. Cars are packed in so tight there's barely room to maneuver and more cars line the street leading up to the restaurant. No way all those people are townies.

I slide my backpack off my shoulder and pull out my camera, snapping a picture. The Polaroid spits out of the camera and I fan it slowly, watching the image come into focus. Fast food has never been so popular.

"I'm going to fill up my entire wall at this rate." I hold the picture up for Gabe and he smiles.

"Guess we're not grabbing fries any time soon."

I glower at the busy restaurant. "Stupid GMA segment."

CHAPTER FIFTEEN

Cheesus on the Line

There's a steady flow of customers at the Gas & Gut Friday night, including a surprising number of out-of-town cars getting gas. The painting in the window appears to be working and I ring up quite a few cheese wheels. I'm sure the *Good Morning America* segment helped.

At a quarter past seven, Mrs. Deardly wanders in. She wears thick glasses with ugly black frames. They must have been her husband's, because they're too big for her thin face and slide down her nose constantly. Her frizzy, yellow-white hair straggles past her ears, and tonight she's dressed in a floral dress with a crisp white collar and a row of faux-pearl buttons down the front.

"Let me know if I can help you with anything," I call out, keeping a close eye on her. Maybe she'll do something suspicious I can add to our suspects notebook. Although, after talking through motives with Gabe, I still can't come up with a single plausible reason Mrs. Deardly would be faking the miracles. Maybe I'm right about her running a meth lab though.

Mrs. D moves to the snack aisle and then the pharmacy aisle. She veers to the right and dithers in front of the tiny shelf containing soup cans, boxed dinners, paper plates, and all the other little sundries people forget or run out of quickly and might remember needing while they fill their gas tanks.

A few minutes later, she sets her selections on the counter in front of me: one bottle of cherry cough syrup, a pack of gum, and one Babybel cheese wheel. My eyebrows shoot up. First time her purchases have varied as long as I've been working here.

"Find everything you need?" I ask.

Mrs. D smiles. "Yes, dear. I thought I'd try one of those cheese rounds. If they're good enough for the Lord after all."

I bite my lip to keep from commenting and ring her up.

On the bright side, Mrs. Deardly doesn't give me a dirty look or make snide comments about my TV appearance. Of all the townies visiting the Gas & Gut that night, she's definitely in the minority in that regard.

Shortly after Mrs. D leaves, Ken wanders in holding a small brown box and wearing his usual dour expression. It morphs into a full-blown scowl as he stops in front of the cash register.

"You trying to run me out of business?" Ken demands.

"No, sir!" I straighten, wondering what I've done now.

Ken hooks a thumb over his shoulder at the front window. "That there cheese wheel has brought in more customers in the past week than we've seen all month. I don't much care if it's a holy relic or not. What I care about is that other people believe that nonsense and are willing to stop in here and buy stuff because of it. So imagine how pleased I am that one of my clerks went on national TV telling the world that cheese wheel is a load of horse shit."

I keep quiet. I'm not apologizing, but I also don't want to say anything that might piss Ken off more and risk my job. If he hasn't decided to fire me already.

"You represent this store, even when you're off duty. That better be your last media interview on the subject," he growls.

I nod. For the first time, I think about how Ken's going to react if I prove the miracles are fake. Based on this conversation, not well. My stomach drops into my toes. I can't lose this job.

Ken plops the box on the counter between us and I eye it warily.

"What's that?"

Ken smiles. It's one of the most terrifying things I've ever seen. He's a certified grump, probably has an official membership card and everything, so anything that has him looking this happy has to be bad. Maybe there's a tiny severed head in the box.

"Find a new place for these," Ken orders, dumping out the black plastic bin closest to the cash register. Two-dozen blue-wrapped chocolate balls go spilling across the counter.

I scramble to catch them, snagging one as it rolls over the edge.

Ken is completely oblivious. He opens the top of the box, pulling out a plastic bag filled with red, pin-back buttons, the kind politicians hand out close to election day. I'm too busy trying to figure out what's going on to worry about the chocolates, so I herd them into a loose pile and resolve to sort them out later.

"Buttons?" I ask, pointing at the bag.

Ken's grin gets even wider. "We're going to sell them for two dollars each." He dumps the buttons into the newly empty bin and plucks one out, handing it to me.

It reads, in blocky, yellow letters, I SAW CHEESUS. You've got to be kidding me.

"Great, aren't they?" Ken says. "Everyone's going to want one. Especially the tourists."

I hold in a laugh with gold-medal-worthy restraint.

Ken stays long enough to tape a small price sticker to the front of the bin, give me one last warning lecture, and then insist I ask each customer if they'd like to buy a button as I ring up their purchases.

Because my day hasn't been crappy enough, Dad calls just before my shift ends. I stare at the phone for a moment, pulling up a mental calendar. Dad always calls late in the evening on the last Sunday of the month for his obligatory "I'm still your parent and I really do give a crap about your life" call. We both know he's only going through the motions. He's a week early and he's got the wrong day.

I consider not answering—Ken does have a no cell phone policy during work hours—but to hell with it. Maybe Dad's decided to head back to Texas.

"Yeah," I say. Not the most gracious greeting but at least I answered. Dad should be grateful he's getting that much out of me.

"Sweet Pea," Dad says. "How are you?"

I wince. Sweet Pea was his nickname for Claire. Geeze. Is the air so thin up in Montana he can't even remember the right nickname? Mine is Buttercup, by the way, and Emmet usually gets Champ. I never said they were great nicknames.

"I'm fine," I grit out. "How's Uncle Carlos?"

Uncle Carlos and my dad's parents, Abuela Silvia and Abuelo Antonio, have lived in Billings, Montana, forever. They stand out in that city like tropical flowers in a field

100

of daisies, but refuse to move back south. Abuelita says she's had enough of the southern summers and prefers a bit of cold. When Dad bolted from Texas, he wound up back in his childhood home. I wonder if my grandparents are pissed he's living in their garage. Dad works with Uncle Carlos now, helping change tires at Carlos's auto shop.

"Carlos is great and so are your grandparents. Abuela sends her love."

There's an awkward silence. I don't do small talk and Dad's never been great at it either.

Finally, he blurts out, "I saw Clemency on the evening news."

I groan and let my head thump against the counter. I guess everyone's heard about our little miracle problem if they're talking about it in the wilds of Montana.

"Peachy," I mutter.

I can hear Dad's frown even through the phone. "There's no need to be sarcastic, Del. I just wanted to know what's going on. *Are* miracles popping up all over town?"

"Yes, Dad. Jesus is strolling down Main Street handing out ice cream cones and lollipops and the Holy Ghost is serving lattes at the coffee shop."

"Del!" Dad snaps. He was raised a strict Roman Catholic, even if he left Catholicism behind when he married Mom. Some things stick with you, though, and in Dad's world, you don't joke about God. Ever.

"What? You saw the news story. I'm sure they covered things. You want to know more? Try coming home."

"You know things are complicated—"

I cut him off. "I'm working. Ken doesn't let us take personal calls on the clock." Before Dad can get in another word I hang up and turn my cell phone off. I hope he doesn't call next week. I've had all the parental quality time I can handle this month.

Chapter Sixteen

Flirting and Blackmail

Sunday, just before noon, Maybelle Jensen totters into the Gas & Gut, white hair swirled on top of her head like an ice cream twist. Her reading glasses cling to the edge of her nose, doing their best to escape. Everything about Maybelle is vague and formless, sagging under the weight of her eighty-three years. Except her eyes. Those are sharp and intelligent. She could turn back a battalion of invading soldiers with a single stare.

I stand behind the cash register, resigned, and wait for Maybelle to launch into a lecture about my lack of church attendance, or more likely that damn interview.

Maybelle smiles and my stomach sinks even lower.

"There you are, Del. I wondered what you were getting up to this morning."

She's so full of it. Everyone in town knew I'd taken the Sunday shift ten minutes after Ken agreed. If gossip is the unofficial town sport, Maybelle is the reigning MVP.

"Your mama was at services with that brother of yours," she continues. "I was surprised you weren't there. Have you seen that amazing cheese wheel? Pastor Stevenson gave a wonderful sermon about how religious signs are God's way of reminding us that he is with us every day in everything we do. God can reach out his finger and make miracles. Our town is blessed."

I smile weakly and nod. "Yes, ma'am, I've seen it." I can't help picturing a giant finger descending from the clouds and poking Clemency, repeatedly. If I laugh, Maybelle will murder me.

Maybelle eyes the display of mini doughnuts and pokes at one of the packages like God's divine finger. "It's positively criminal that you weren't able to attend services this morning. I should talk to Ken about closing the store on Sundays. It's the Lord's day, after all."

Horror holds me still a moment too long and Maybelle swings her gaze back to me, frowning at my lack of response.

"Coffee?" I squeak. Without waiting for an answer, I dash for the coffee machine and fill a cup. If she scalds her tongue off, she won't be able to talk to Ken.

"Aren't you sweet."

"No charge," I add.

"Now that wouldn't be right, dear. I'll pay for my coffee like anyone else. Add a cheese wheel to my order and one of those bear claws."

"I'm sorry, we're out of Babybels again. Can't keep the things in stock, they go so fast. There should be more tomorrow. Would you like a button?"

I snatch up a button and contemplate stabbing her with it.

Maybelle eyes the garish design and shakes her head. "I wouldn't want to put holes in my Sunday best, but thank you for offering." She pauses by the door after I've rung her up. "I won't forget to talk to Ken for you. I'm sure a bit of guidance from Pastor Stevenson would go a long way toward helping you see the miracles for what they are. It's so easy to get mixed up when you're young."

The door clatters shut behind her and I glare at it, trying to melt the glass.

"Easy to get mixed up when you're young," I mutter under my breath. "I knew she couldn't resist lecturing me about that interview."

Stupid Maybelle, always getting in everyone's business. She carries a lot of weight in this town and it's not all stuffed under her floral muumuus. Her grandfather was the original town founder. Thanks to that and her spot on the town council, Maybelle's managed to strong-arm a lot of people. If she corners Ken about my Sunday shift, there's no doubt I'll be hearing about it.

By the time Andy breezes in at ten till eight, I've stopped glaring at the freezer case and I've sold four pins. I'm also bored out of my mind.

"How's it hanging?" Andy asks, leaning against the counter. "Any excitement?"

I snort. "As if anything interesting ever happens."

"There was the cheese wheel," Andy says.

I nod grudgingly. "Was Wendy telling the truth in that ABC interview? Are you back at St. Andrew's?"

Andy drops his gaze and becomes very interested in the button display. "Uncle Bobby can be persuasive when he wants."

I narrow my eyes. Perhaps Maybelle isn't the only one strong-arming people in town. I wonder what Bobby said to convince Andy to attend services again. Must be some new argument because I'm sure he tried them all when Andy stopped going two years ago and declared himself an atheist. Could Bobby have persuaded Andy to plant that cheese wheel at the Gas & Gut in the first place and now he's using it to blackmail his nephew?

There aren't any customers in the store. Might as well take advantage of the lag while it lasts. If I ask Andy some questions about the cheese wheel, maybe he'll slip up and confess everything.

"It's pretty lucky you finding that cheese wheel," I begin.

Andy frowns and rubs the back of his neck. "Yeah, guess so. Course, you're the one who almost bought the thing. Could have been you holding the miracle cheese."

I haven't let myself dwell on that thought, but it's hovered in the back of my mind. If Andy hadn't been goofing around, I'd have taken that cheese wheel home and Emmet probably would have snarfed it without looking twice. No Baby Cheesus. No miracle mania. Funny how one decision can change everything. But if Andy planted the cheese wheel, he would've made sure he was the one to open it. How do I even know the cheese wheel he opened is the same one I tried to buy? He could've switched them when I stepped out of the store.

I force a laugh. "So close to greatness, yet so far." I mentally scramble, trying to find a way to ask him about the cheese wheel without outright accusing him of planting it. There isn't one and I don't want to tip my hand too soon. Instead I switch gears.

"When you unwrapped Baby Cheesus, was there anything weird about the wax covering the cheese wheel?"

"Weird how?"

"I don't know. Did the wax feel different? Were there any marks on the wax? Was it the same red as the other cheeses? Was the little pull tab thingy fixed all the way down in the wax or was it sticking up?" I've been thinking up questions for days and they all tumble out.

106

I desperately want to grab a notebook and pencil, but I figure that might frighten Andy off. If he did fake the miracles he's not going to want me writing down info that might incriminate him. But he might answer my questions if I catch him off guard.

I prop my hands under my chin, smile flirtatiously, and stare at him like he's the most fascinating thing in the world. "Well?" I prompt gently.

"That's a lot of questions." Andy sounds shell-shocked.

I shrug and try to act casual. Andy's eyes drop to my chest and I hold in a grimace. "So anything weird?"

"Hmmm," Andy's eyes snap back to mine and his cheeks redden. "No. It was just like every other Babybel. Nothing special until I opened it."

"Thanks," I murmur, hiding my disappointment. He could be lying, but unless I find a spare polygraph machine lying around there's no way to tell for sure.

"You got plans for later?" Andy asks.

I stop smiling. Damn, I must be better at flirting than I thought. "No, but you do. Night shift, remember?"

"Yeah, yeah. Want to keep me company?"

"Stick around this place for another couple hours? Are you nuts?"

"Possibly. Come on, it's not that long and I hate Sunday nights, they're always slow. I will die of boredom if you don't take pity on me." Andy grabs my hand, widening his eyes and hamming it up.

I force out a strained laugh and yank my hand away. "Sorry. I've got a paper due and Gabe's picking me up." Over Andy's shoulder, I spot Gabe's car with a sigh of relief. "Looks like he's here already. I better dash."

Andy drops the joking manner and nods. "Okay, no big deal."

As I slide into the passenger seat, Gabe glances between me and Andy, just visible behind the main counter. "Something going on between you two?" There's a little growl in his voice and it makes my stomach flip over. He can't actually be jealous.

"Nah, we were only goofing around."

"If you say so." He doesn't sound entirely convinced, but he loosens his hold on the steering wheel.

I settle back in my seat, propping my feet on the dashboard, and pull my notebook out of my backpack. "We can go over notes on the way to your place. Andy says he didn't notice anything odd about the cheese wheel when he opened it."

"If there's a pretty girl around, Andy wouldn't notice a gorilla in a tutu dancing in front of him." Gabe's voice still sounds weird and did he just call me pretty?

I try not to read too much into that. Gabe's just acting strange because he thinks Andy's too much of a player to be hooking up with his best friend. I can't tell Gabe I was only flirting to get information out of Andy, though. Just admitting that to myself makes me feel low. How far *am* I willing to go to prove the miracles are fake?

Monday evening my cell phone rings. When I check the display, I find the Gas & Gut's number. I don't have a shift today and I'm pretty sure I didn't burn down the store last time I was there. Maybe it's Andy calling to flirt some more? Although I really, really hope not.

I answer with a cautious "Hello?"

"Del?" Ken's voice rasps over the line. "We gotta talk."

My stomach drops into my toes. Maybelle must have followed through on her threat. Ken's going to fire me. It's that or the store is closing down. Or . . . I mentally flail searching for another reason Ken would call. I didn't even know he had my number. He must have looked it up on my employee paperwork.

"About what, sir?" I have never called Ken sir before. Maybe it'll earn me brownie points.

"Some people are making noise about having a kid working so many hours and especially on Sunday mornings."

"I only work twenty hours a week!" I'd work more if Ken would let me.

He grumbles under his breath before continuing, "We both know it's the Sunday shift causing all this fuss. Fact is, I don't want the Gas & Gullet closed on Sundays—we need the money. Even with sales up thanks to Baby Cheesus, that damned Exxon is still stealing most of the customers coming off the highway. The last thing I need is the town biddies picketing my place 'cause I'm oppressing minors. I had enough of that this summer."

A few months ago, Maybelle went door to door with a petition to get the Gas & Gut to stop selling cigarettes. She has no traction with the Exxon because it's corporate, but the Gas & Gut doesn't have fancy lawyers defending it. Maybelle only got fifty signatures on her petition so she and a few of the other seniors picketed the store. There's something about little old ladies chanting in unison that is downright terrifying. The Gas & Gut didn't see much business that week and Ken quickly gave in.

"Please—" I begin, but Ken cuts me off.

"We're gonna open at ten on Sundays starting this week. That'll keep Maybelle and her senior terror squad off my back."

I slump against the wall behind my bed, glad I'm already sitting. At least I'm not fired.

Ken clears his throat and adopts his "I'm the boss" tone of voice. "I don't need no more trouble, you understand? You better be at church Sunday morning. Make sure Maybelle doesn't feel the need to come visit me about my ungodly store clerks."

"Yes, sir," I mumble.

CHAPTER SEVENTEEN

The Politics of Miracles

The house is dark and quiet when I get home after my shift Tuesday night. Gabe has to study for his advanced history test so I'm on my lonesome. My plans are grand and wild: a bowl of Rocky Road ice cream and some quality time with my notes on the miracles. I thought up a few questions I want to ask Pastor Bobby when I have a chance.

Mom's already at work and Emmet's disappeared again. The answering machine light is flashing so I pause and hit play. There are three new messages.

Maybelle's strident voice crackles from the machine, cut by static thanks to our crappy phone line. "Gena, we need to talk about Delaney and what she's been getting up to. I'm sure you know about her unfortunate interview last week. Them news folks are running it again and stirring up all sorts of trouble. Now I know you've been distracted since little Claire passed, and God knows I sympathize. It's been fifty years since my Janey died and there are still days it's hard to get out of bed. No mother should ever lose a child. But you have to control Delaney before that girl shames this entire town. Saying such things on TV. I thought it would pass but it's ju—" Beep. Maybelle is cut off mid-word.

What the hell? I stare at the machine like it's going to jump up and bite me.

The next message begins, Maybelle again, this time sounding not just pissed but exasperated. "Call me. First thing tomorrow. Maybe Delaney can call that reporter and offer to do a new interview, talk about how these miracles are a sign of God's blessings on our town." Beep.

Message number three is even worse. Mayor Thompson's deep, concerned voice says, "Gena? You there?" A moment of silence, then, "Please call me first thing in the morning. We need to talk about Del and damage control. I'm sure you know all about the current situation." Beep.

The machine helpfully informs me there are no new messages. The ones we have are bad enough. I consider deleting them, but I know Maybelle, at least, will keep calling until she reaches Mom.

What happened? Why are they freaking out about my interview now, days later?

My cell phone rings and I answer without checking. Stupid. Thank goodness it's just Gabe.

"Did you watch the ten o'clock news?" he asks. It must be dire if he isn't even bothering with a hello.

"I get all the current events I need from Mr. Rayburn's class."

Gabe sighs. "Guess who was featured in one of the lead stories?"

"Wendy?" I ask in a small voice. But I already know the answer.

"Oh, they re-aired Wendy's interview as well, parts of it anyway. But you got top billing. They led with you say-ing the miracles are fakes and then they brought in some experts to comment on the likelihood that the miracles are real. There was a guy from the Vatican and everything."

"What was the consensus?"

"Because none of the parties involved are Catholic and Clemency doesn't even have a Catholic church, the Vatican isn't taking a stand either way. There was some preacher from Nebraska, a televangelist I think, and he said the miracles seem genuine. Then there was this other guy, I can't remember his credentials, sorry, who said they had to be fake."

"Has that televangelist even been to Clemency?" I demand, muttering under my breath.

"Don't think so. But with the number of people passing through town lately, who can tell?"

He pauses and for a long minute it's just the sound of our breath over the line.

Yeah, I'm glad other people are calling bullshit on the miracles, but that news story tonight is going to cause trouble. I glance at the answering machine. Is already causing trouble. If the entire town is out to get me, it's going to make investigating hard. But maybe I won't need to investigate anymore. Maybe that news segment will shame the town into dropping this whole miracle nonsense. Except I still want to know who did it and why.

There's a burning knot of curiosity and anger in my chest and it won't go away until I find the truth. If I can prove the miracles are fake, if I can find out who's planting them, maybe things will start to make sense again. Maybe life can swing back to normal for me and everyone else.

"You still awake over there?" Gabe asks quietly.

"Yeah, still here. This doesn't change anything. At least not for me. If you want to back out, though . . ."

Gabe makes a disgusted noise. "You're not getting rid of me that easily. Besides, the news segment gave me an idea. I want to look up how the Vatican determines if a miracle is genuine. Maybe we can use that to settle things one way or another."

"Maybe," I murmur. It's a good idea, actually. If you believe in miracles. "Want to have a Google-off after school tomorrow?"

Gabe laughs and agrees. We chat for a few more minutes and then hang up. The red light on the answering machine glares up at me with malevolent persistence. Tomorrow is going to be interesting.

The next morning, when I step out the front door, Mayor Thompson is waiting for me with one foot on the first stair of our front porch. I freeze in the middle of pulling on my backpack.

"Ah, Del," he says, peering past me into the entry hall. "I was hoping to talk with your mother." His eyes shift back to me and he looks uncomfortable.

"She's sleeping. Probably only got home an hour ago." I keep my voice neutral.

Mayor Thompson dithers, stepping back so he's not straddling the stair anymore, and smooths a hand down the side of his slacks. It's a nervous gesture at odds with his sleek appearance. He's dressed in a button-down dress shirt, cuff links at his wrists, shiny black shoes gleaming obscenely next to the caked dirt covering our porch.

Normally Mayor Thompson is all smiles, a born politician. Today he looks like he got caught with a prostitute on his lap and the story's about to go viral.

"I see. Perhaps I should—but you're here and—" He falls silent before sighing and then continues, "I suppose, given everything, it's best to talk to you directly." He doesn't look happy about it, but stiffens his shoulders and nods. "Yes. That'd be best. Can we go inside, please?"

"I have to get to school. Mom will be up in a couple hours if you want to try calling her." I try to deflect him back onto Mom. If he complains to her about me she'll probably forget by the time I get home, no discussion necessary.

Mayor Thompson shakes his head. "No, I'd rather get this over with. I'll call Cheryl and let her know you'll be late."

Cheryl is the school principal, Mrs. Candlewhite. The last thing I need is the two of them having a long chat about me. What if Mrs. Candlewhite decides to put me in detention for the rest of the year? I'm sure she could come up with a reason. The fact I have a dead sister is the only thing that saved me from being suspended last year after I started a couple fights. Ruining Clemency's miracle claims, however, probably trumps the dead sister card.

Just then, Emmet comes barreling through the front door and almost knocks me over. He has a piece of toast shoved halfway in his mouth and his cell phone pressed to his ear. He stumbles to a halt, his arm banging against mine. I give him an annoyed glare.

Emmet looks from me to Mayor Thompson, frowning. He spits out the toast and mumbles, "Gotta go," into the phone, then snaps it closed. Emmet's cheeks flush and he quickly shoves the phone into his back pocket when he catches me eyeing it curiously. "What's going on?"

Mayor Thompson steps forward and slaps Emmet on the shoulder. "Excellent game last Friday, son. You were a powerhouse. Keep playing like that and you'll have your pick of scholarships."

"Thanks." Emmet's on familiar territory and the flush quickly fades. My brother can talk football 24/7. "I certainly hope I can land a scholarship, sir. Can we help you with something?"

Mayor Thompson gives a fake chuckle. "I just need a moment of Delaney's time. I'll drop her off at school, afterward."

Emmet narrows his eyes. "I'll wait."

Part of me wants to tell Emmet off for his ridiculous over-protective big brother act. The other half wants to hug him. I'm not sure what he thinks Mayor Thompson is going to do, but the fact that he wants to protect me from it is kind of endearing.

Mayor Thompson's smile dies, and he gives a resigned nod. "Fine, fine. Can we go inside, please? I abhor lingering on doorsteps."

I reluctantly lead the way inside and the three of us take seats around the kitchen table. This isn't a comfy couch sort of conversation.

"Maybe I should get Mom," Emmet says, glancing up at the ceiling.

I put a hand on his arm. "Let her sleep. I know what this is about."

Mayor Thompson looks surprised. "Do you? That makes things a bit easier."

"Can someone clue me in?" Emmet asks, sounding annoyed.

"ABC ran a new story on the miracles last night. My interview was kind of the centerpiece," I say. "They called in experts and it turns out I'm not the only one who thinks the miracles are fishy."

Mayor Thompson's lips tighten and he doesn't look as nervous and unsure anymore. "That news piece could be extremely harmful to this town. Since word of the miracles has spread we've had more tourist traffic through town than ever. Almost all of the local businesses are benefiting from increased patronage, more sales. I expect even more interest in the miracles as people return home and talk about them. If the number of visitors keeps up, we might even build a permanent display, cater to pilgrim traffic. The miracles have been good for our town and having one of our citizens disparage that is disgraceful and un-civic. Your interview could undo all the good we've seen. No one wants to come see a fake miracle. No one wants to listen to a teenage girl spew ridiculous accusations. We need to come together as a community, not cause dissension."

I wonder if he practiced that speech in the mirror. Looked up some big words to throw in the middle. It sounds impressive. But I'm not going to be intimidated by a man who still has his mom iron his underwear. I heard two of the old ladies laughing about it at a church social last year.

Emmet answers before I have a chance. "Del already gave that interview. There's nothing she can do about it now."

"She can keep away from any more reporters and stop spreading rumors about the miracles being fake," Mayor Thompson fires back. "I don't want so much as a line in the school paper hinting about it."

"Or what?" I demand. "Freedom of speech is a thing, you know."

"You're a minor," Mayor Thompson snaps. "You should think before you speak. There are plenty of community

117

service projects around town that could use a hand. I imagine that might interfere with your work schedule."

Great, now even the mayor is threatening my job. The thing is, I can only be pushed so far. I get up and lean forward, planting both of my hands on the table, eyes fixed on Mayor Thompson. "Maybe the miracles are real, but I doubt it. I have a right to know the truth."

Emmet puts a hand on my shoulder, easing me back. "Don't borrow trouble, Del," he mutters. He focuses on the mayor. "Del's taken Claire's death hard. With the anniversary coming up . . ." He lets his voice trail away, playing the pity angle.

I shrug his hand away and whirl on my brother. "Don't you dare bring Claire into this!"

Emmet shakes his head and gives Mayor Thompson a look like *See what I mean?*

My brother's phone rings and I snatch it up before he has a chance, flipping it open. "He's busy right now, I'm sure he's available for a booty call later."

The color drains from Emmet's face. I snap the phone closed and fling it at him.

What I want to do is throw it at Mayor Thompson, but that would give him the perfect excuse to assign me community service.

"You've said what you wanted," I tell the mayor. "I'm sure you don't want to make me any later than I am, even with that call to Mrs. Candlewhite." I give my brother a scathing look. "I'll be in the car."

Ten minutes later, we're on the road and Emmet's mouth is a thin, furious line. "Don't touch my phone again."

"Worried I'll scare off your girlfriend?"

He glances away from the road long enough to study my face. For some reason I can't fathom, he relaxes. He still looks pissed, but less likely to go all road warrior and kill us both with his insane driving. He eases back on the gas pedal slightly as we pull out of our neighborhood. "You're great at screwing things up, you know that?"

I turn away from him so he can't see the hit he just scored. I think of the last words I said to Claire and everything that's happened since. Emmet doesn't know how right he is.

CHAPTER EIGHTEEN

Another Suspect for the List

We were half an hour late leaving the house and it doesn't look like we're getting to school any time soon. For the first time in the history of Clemency, there's a traffic jam on Main Street. And it isn't because of an accident.

The car ahead of us has a New York license plate and more bumper stickers than should be legal. I'm pretty sure the stickers are the only things holding that bumper in place. Rust Bucket inches along at a pace slower than Emmet fixing his hair in the morning.

We don't see the problem until we draw level with McDonald's. The parking lot is packed and one of the town cops is waving angry motorists past. New signs in front of the building next door say PARKING FOR FEED & SEED CUSTOMERS ONLY!!! VIOLATORS WILL BE TOWED! I'm not sure where the Feed & Seed is going to get a tow truck, but the parking sign has four exclamation points so they mean business.

The cars that can't get into the McDonald's lot are circling the block and clogging up traffic even more. Some people must have given up and parked along the street in nearby neighborhoods because there's a lot of foot traffic as well.

"Guess Mayor Thompson doesn't need to worry about my interview chasing off tourists."

Emmet curses under his breath and hits the steering wheel, glaring at the car in front of us. "This is ridiculous."

"Couldn't agree more," I say sweetly.

Emmet curses again and smacks his horn. The guy in the car ahead of us twists in his seat, looks Emmet right in the eye, and flips him off. My brother falls silent. This has to be a first. Road rage is unheard of in Clemency and you just don't go around giving strangers the finger. We've got manners. Mostly.

"Damn out-of-towners," Emmet snarls. He gives the guy the finger in return and hits his horn again. Before either of them can take their little pissing match to the next level, traffic moves forward and New York switches on his turn signal as though he's going to be the one car the cop lets in the McDonald's lot. He isn't, but New York turns anyway, stopping beside the cop and rolling down his window to begin arguing.

Emmet pulls past him, glaring, whips around a white Toyota, and then plays a game of chicken with several cars attempting to get back onto Main Street. We hit the school parking lot minutes later. Emmet's breathing fast and we're now an hour late.

Should I say something to try to calm him down? Gloat about all the trouble the miracles are causing? Slink away while I can?

I opt for silence when Emmet smacks the steering wheel again. As I get out, Emmet says, "Keep away from Mayor Thompson and try not to piss anyone else off."

"Love you too, bro." I make sure to slam my door with a little extra force.

I don't see Gabe until lunch. He's standing by his locker, peering down the hall and checking faces. He smiles when he sees me. "Hey. Wondered what happened to you. You haven't skipped class in a while."

"It wasn't intentional." I stop beside him and wait as he gets his lunch bag.

"I've got a new suspect for the list," I say.

Gabe quirks an eyebrow so I tell him about Mayor Thompson's visit that morning.

"Maybe we *should* back off and leave things alone." He closes his locker and twists the lock into place. "It's not worth losing your job."

"I'm not going to lose my job. We'll be careful. No one other than you knows I'm trying to prove the miracles are fake, right? The only thing they know is that I talked to a reporter. But so did Wendy."

Gabe's mouth twists. "Wendy isn't on the mayor's hit list."

"Please, he doesn't have a hit list. But you have to admit, he's got tons of motive."

"Yeah. I'll give you that point. But you should take his threats seriously. If he puts you on community service, Ken's going to have to replace you at the store."

"Like I said, we'll be stealthy. No one will even know we're looking into things. Besides, I have you helping me and who'd suspect the preacher's son of helping disprove the miracles?"

Gabe sputters. "I'm not helping disprove them. It's just as likely we'll find evidence that they're real."

I wave his words away. It's a minor point. He's help-ing investigate, whatever he tells himself, and that's what matters. But there's a bigger threat to my continued employment than Mayor Thompson's hissy fit this morning. Ken's ultimatum is still hanging over my head.

"Would you mind if I came to services on Sunday? Ken switched up my hours," I blurt out.

Gabe's mouth drops open, but he quickly clamps it shut. He can't keep the shock out of his voice, however. "You serious?"

"As a heart attack. I figure you could use the attendance bump. Besides, you've been asking me to go for years."

It's true. He's never pressured me, but he's dropped enough hints that I know he wants me to see his dad in action. Gabe says his dad is the best preacher in the entire southern United States. I'm thinking Gabe's a bit biased, but I've always been curious. I like the feeling of peace, of absolute stillness, inside Holy Cross when Gabe and I clean up Sunday nights. Maybe I can find a bit of that peace during the day, something I haven't found at St. Andrew's in a long time. If I'm going to be forced into attending services, I'm going to do it on my terms.

"I'd love for you to come," Gabe says.

I smile and shove down a tiny surge of guilt at how happy he looks. Gabe would understand if I told him about Ken and Maybelle, I'm sure of it. But I don't say a word.

That afternoon, things take a bizarre turn in history class. When Mr. Rayburn walks in, he's cradling his right hand against his chest like it's been scalded. He ignores our curious stares and points at the whiteboard with his left hand, to a quote filling the top half: *The educated differ from the uneducated as much as the living from the dead.*

"To whom is this quote attributed?" Mr. Rayburn asks.

No one answers. He waits, eyes moving over us. When it's obvious no one is going to volunteer an answer, he sighs. "If you had done last night's reading assignment, every single one of you would have the answer."

Wayne's hand shoots into the air and Mr. Rayburn frowns. Wayne never raises his hand.

"Mr. Hissep?"

"What's wrong with your hand?" Wayne asks.

There's a low snicker from the other jocks in the room.

Mr. Rayburn glowers and tucks his hand closer against his chest. "While that is none of your business, it's clear none of you are going to focus on our lesson while you're busy gawking at my hand." He raises his right hand, like he's saluting, slides his cuff up his arm several inches, and then waits expectantly.

The room is as quiet as when he first walked in. I don't see anything wrong with his arm. My classmates look just as confused.

Mr. Rayburn huffs out an exasperated breath and points at a large mole on his wrist. "This morning I discovered this mole. It's shaped like a cross. I've been touched by God."

You've got to be kidding me. Mr. Rayburn is covered in so many moles and brown spots he looks like an off-color Dalmatian. How would he even notice a new one? And a cross-shaped mole? Gross. But it's clear Mr. Rayburn thinks something divine has happened because he's proudly waving his arm around and beaming at the class.

"I don't want anyone to be distracted by this latest miracle, however, so let's please try to focus on the lesson."

The jocks are snickering again, and I have to agree with them. But, while this definitely qualifies as weird, Mr. Rayburn isn't the first person in town claiming a so-called personal miracle. They've been cropping up everywhere.

Two days ago Kit Spencer, the librarian, said she saw an image of the Holy Ghost in her bathroom mirror after her evening shower. Naturally by the time she'd grabbed her camera it had already faded. But she swears it was there. That same day, Andrew Carol, our quarterback, found a four-leaf clover on the practice field. I'm willing to admit there may be a miracle in there somewhere because I wasn't aware Andrew could count that high. Yesterday morning, no less than three freshman girls all said that God spoke to them while they were in the girls' bathroom. Of course, they also admitted he told them panties were optional clothing so I'm betting on a prank rather than any sort of divine fashion tips. Miraculous recoveries? Please. Half the town is claiming one of those—from cured colds to mysteriously disappearing allergies.

The epidemic of crazy in this town is definitely on the rise.

I don't work Wednesday nights, so there's plenty of time for Gabe and me to have our Google-off. I pull my laptop out and sit on the floor in Gabe's family room. He scoots his chair closer to the desk, cracks his knuckles, and then powers up the ancient computer.

"Ready?" I ask casually, already pulling a search engine up.

Gabe grins. "Absolutely."

"Ready, set"—I tense, fingers poised—"go!"

Gabe's hands fly across the keyboard and the *tap-tap* of keys fills the air.

I begin with the search term "holy food." All that gets me are a bunch of recipes and some suggestions on restaurants close to Houston. The image hits seem more promising, however. There's a weird-looking Cheeto and Jesus's face in a frying pan. I click to view the full image results page and immediately regret it. Dog-wearing-a-bib I can totally handle. What that guy is doing to a Hot Pocket, on the other hand . . . I may need therapy by the end of this.

A few more clicks bring me to a page filled with pictures of the supposed face of Jesus on various food and food-related items. Man, that guy gets around. Interesting, but not terribly helpful in the hoax-proving department.

Gabe crows and pumps his fist in the air. "Score! Once again, my Google-fu kicks your butt."

"Please! I could smoke you any day of the week. What have you got?"

"Oh, just a list of the six requirements the Vatican uses to determine if a miracle is genuine."

Damn. Round one to Gabe. I remain gracious. "Spit it out, then." Fine, gracious might not be the right word, but I'm being provoked; that fist pump was totally unnecessary.

"One, the facts of the case have to be error free. Two, the person receiving the message or miracle has to be of sound mind, moral fiber, and recognize the church's authority."

"You realize Baby Cheesus doesn't hold up to requirement number two, right? I don't think Andy recognizes anyone's authority and his morals are definitely questionable."

Gabe scowls at me. "Do you want to hear the list or not?"

"Yeah, yeah."

"Three, the miracle can't claim Jesus, God, Mary, or one of the saints says something that is against church doctrine. Four, any claims made involving the miracle can't contradict church doctrine. Five, making money can't be a motive in the miracle's discovery. Six, the miracle must result in religious devotion, or acts of devotion, that aren't a result of mass hysteria."

"See, that last one right there. I think you're making my case for me again. Definite mass hysteria moments happening."

"But the miracles have brought religious pilgrims to town, church attendance is up, and there have been healings. So requirement number six is in the bag."

"We'll have to agree to disagree on that one. But seriously, back to the moral fiber thing. You can't argue that one. And this many miracles so close together? There's no way!"

"It's definitely a bit weird. The miracles could still be real, though. What did you find?"

While Gabe is talking I enter a few new search terms and score a win. "How about this. There's a phenomenon called pareidolia. It's basically the fact that people's brains are hardwired to recognize faces so we see them even when they're not there. The whole man in the moon thing? Or that face on Mars? Baby Cheesus and McJesus are like that. Our brains are just misfiring."

"That would blow your whole conspiracy theory right out of the water. Even if they're both natural phenomena, that doesn't mean they aren't miraculous."

"It doesn't mean they are though."

We're at a stalemate again.

CHAPTER NINETEEN

Gather All Ye Faithful

S unday morning, I drag myself out of bed and stare dolefully at my closet. I pull out a couple shirts, none of which feature cartoon characters, settle on one, and then grab a nice pair of slacks. After the service, I'll need to head straight to work and there won't be time to change. I'm not stocking shelves and scrubbing down the soda machine in a skirt.

Mom is sitting at the dining room table nursing a coffee when I get downstairs. I tiptoe past but she turns and catches me, frowning at my outfit. "Don't you have a dress for services?"

How the hell does Mom know I'm headed to church and not work? She must have rejoined the town gossip chain. Maybelle's probably telling everyone who'll listen how she's saving my soul by making me attend church again.

I pause with one hand on the front door, looking back at her. "This is fine."

Mom gets up and straightens the pale blue sundress she's wearing. "Let me grab the keys and we'll head out."

"I can walk." The words are sharper then I meant and Mom flinches, but pastes on a smile.

"Don't be silly, what would people think if we didn't arrive together?"

"I'm not going to St. Andrew's."

Mom glances at my black slacks and cream top, eyebrows drawing together. "But—"

"I'm going to Holy Cross."

Her mouth forms a little *oh*. "But they're Baptist!"

She says it like Baptist is a four-letter word and I'm off to cavort naked and sacrifice a goat. I can't help laughing. Mom's shocked expression dissolves into a glare.

"Did Gabe talk you into this? You belong at St. Andrew's with your family."

I cross my arms over my chest, holding in a sigh. "My choice, Mom." Before she can protest again I duck out the front door and pull it closed behind me.

The streets are busy despite the early hour. Moms in floral hats, little girls in frilly dresses, and dads in casual suits walk or drive on their way to church. Most of the cars are headed to St. Andrew's, and there's a traffic jam in the parking lot. I turn toward Holy Cross on the opposite side of town.

The St. Andrew's bell rings triumphantly and Holy Cross's speakers sound tiny and small in comparison, the gospel song more plaintive than enticing. It's a good fifteen-minute walk to Holy Cross and I pop headphones into my ears, turning on the latest track from Screech Monkey. The noise washes away the world and it's just me and the crash of drums, the snarling wail of a guitar. The lyrics are an unintelligible rush of syllables and I relax, not having to think about anything.

When I finally reach Holy Cross, I feel weird stepping inside for an actual service. Like I might burst into flames or giant angels will appear barring my way and saying, "Halt, unbeliever." Neither happens. The reality is much worse.

Gabe is waiting at the front of the church, greeting people as they come in and handing out programs for the morning service. His face lights up with a huge smile when he sees me. I am a fake. A phony. The absolute worst friend in the entire world. I should have told him the truth about why I asked to come this morning.

"I didn't think you'd show," Gabe says, still smiling.

He hands me a green printed paper. On the front, a dove rises from a group of clouds, and the date is printed below: Sunday, September 24.

"And yet here I am. Where should I sit?" I curl the program into a tight tube and fiddle with the edge, glancing past Gabe at the greeting area and the sanctuary beyond with its rows of pews. The rooms look so different with morning sunlight streaming inside and people milling around.

Gabe gestures at the sanctuary. "First row, on the right. I always sit there."

I smile nervously and shuffle inside.

"I'll be there in a few minutes, just have to finish passing these out." He hands a program to a couple standing behind me and they begin chatting.

St. Andrew's has padded seats on their pews, a lush tapestry-like material that's all puffy and still somehow uncomfortable. Holy Cross's pews are bare wood, red-brown with a bright lacquered finish. I pass down the regimented rows. Half are empty.

Audrey Mills, one of those old people who always seems to be around, is perched at the church organ, enthusiastically punching out a tune. Ellen Martin stands beside her wearing a purple and gold choir robe so wide it could double as a church tent.

Ellen's cheeks are flushed as she sings for all she's worth into a tiny silver microphone. In the pew across from me, two old ladies nod along with the music, one of them knitting a neon green scarf. I've never seen anyone knitting at St. Andrew's.

I glance at the other people in the sanctuary and spot a baseball cap in the back row. A few people are casually dressed, others decked out like Jesus is holding a reception and they're the guests of honor.

At the front of the church the piano falls silent and Ellen puts down the microphone. Gabe slides in next to me a moment later. On cue, Reverend Beaudean steps up to the podium, a smile pasted on. His cheeks look sunken and worry lines tug at the corners of his mouth and crisscross his forehead. He takes a deep breath and his eyes sweep the sanctuary, taking in everyone. The lines deepen.

"Welcome on this fine and beautiful morning," Reverend Beaudean begins. "I know that many of you have seen the miracles that have been visited on our town."

The word "miracles" surprises me, considering Reverend Beaudean was yelling at Bobby about setting up a sideshow last week. Sure, the Reverend tried to get McJesus, but he can't actually think it's a miracle, can he? The rest of his sermon quickly proves me wrong.

"We live in miraculous times," the reverend continues. "I am grateful to be here, at this moment. To be a part of something truly extraordinary. These humble signs point us back to our Father and to his service. But there is a danger in those signs as well. If we focus on them, and not the one who sent them, then we worship falsely.

God is the center of our faith and how we worship him should not falter in the face of such miracles. Go and see the image, this McJesus, as it's being called. Whether you believe in it or not, you must believe in the Maker, Our Lord, who through his compassion and love saves us. Let us take glory in Our Heavenly Father and his unending love. Let us remain true to Him."

Several people in the congregation nod and I hear a heartfelt "Amen" from the back of the room. The sermon rolls on with Reverend Beaudean talking about faith and belief, about what miracles mean to each of us.

Gabe's face shines as he watches his father, hanging on every word. Did I ever look like that, watching my parents? Before our family fell apart? My dad was a mechanic, the king of cars. He could fix anything. My mom was master of a thousand things—able to fix cuts with a kiss, make bake sale cupcakes with no notice, and lull a scared little girl to sleep at night with a story. They were giants when I was young, invincible. Until they weren't. Until they couldn't fix anything. Not Claire, not our family, and not even themselves. Their prayers and their faith weren't enough to save anyone.

Gabe touches my elbow, urging me up, and I focus on the service again. Everyone is standing and the first notes of a hymn come from the church organ. Gabe frowns at me, looking concerned, but I shake my head. I can't say all the things I want. I thought coming here, I'd be able to see things through his eyes. Discover some secret that I've missed. But faith is a gulf I'm not sure we'll ever bridge.

All these people, maybe they believe in God even more because of the miracles. I think of Mom, across town at St. Andrews, probably staring at Baby Cheesus and fixating on Claire. Some lies are tiny and small, they don't hurt anyone, and some lies are so big they tear apart families and lives.

The songs go on forever, five in a row. I stare at a battered hymnal, words catching in my throat. Beside me, Gabe's hands are free—no hymnal needed because he knows the songs by heart.

"Go with God," Reverend Beaudean says after the last song ends. All around us people shuffle and gather their things, edging out of the pews.

Gabe glances at the sanctuary doors, but remains in place, laser-focused on me. "So, what did you think? Great sermon, right?"

I nod and smile, putting on a show for Gabe. He's clearly hoping one sermon's going to make me reconsider my whole "God doesn't give a shit" attitude. Sorry, bud. But he looks so eager, I say, "Your dad's amazing."

Gabe beams.

Reverend Beaudean stands twenty feet away, cornered by half a dozen people all vying for his attention. He patiently listens to each one and pats an arm or offers a smile, a concerned frown.

Gabe mutters "Damn" under his breath. I turn to see what he's looking at and notice the trickle of water snaking down the wall in the far corner. Gabe hurries to the front of the room and pulls a bucket and a wad of towels from behind the altar. I join him and help mop up the small puddle that's already formed on the warped wooden floor. We position the bucket and use it to hold more towels in place. It's a temporary measure at best; the towels will have to be switched out in a few minutes.

"There weren't even any clouds this morning. Maybe it'll just be a quick storm." He glances furtively at the handful of people still in the room and then catches Reverend Beaudean's eye and nods his head at the bucket.

His dad's shoulders slump and he nods back.

"Need more supplies?" I ask Gabe, holding up the last few towels.

"Yeah. We've got a pile of extra towels in Dad's office. Can you grab them?"

"Sure thing."

I jog to the row of offices in the back of the building. While the rest of the church is shabby but clean, Mr. Beaudean's office looks like an episode of *Hoarders*. There are boxes piled in the corners, books and papers litter every surface, and three coffee cups are on his desk, one on its side leaking coffee sludge over several envelopes.

Not a towel in sight. Taking a deep breath, I plunge inside.

The papers and ecclesiastical books I expected. The egg decorating kit on the other hand, not so much. I shift a couple of boxes and glance beneath them, before surrendering to the inevitable and opening each box in turn. There's a box filled with toilet paper rolls. Another has a mishmash of tools, a small soldering iron, and some tiny jars of wood stain. A few wood chips and part of a wood slat lay beside them. In the box beneath that I discover a leather-working kit, complete with awls and metal stamps. Is this Gabe's old junk? I swear we used that leather kit back in sixth grade to make ourselves a couple holsters for our water guns.

Finally, in the fifth box, I find the towels.

"Can I help you find something, Del?"

I jump and turn back to the door. Reverend Beaudean is standing in the hall, frowning in at me. His cheeks are flushed and he darts a glance at the mess covering his desk, the boxes I've already searched. Guess he wasn't keen for anyone to see what a wreck his office is.

I plunge a hand into the box and pull out a wad of terrycloth, holding the towels up for him to see. "Just looking for these."

He doesn't move.

"For the leak?" I add. "Gabe and I are trying to mop up the water before it does any more damage."

The frown disappears and Mr. Beaudean nods, smoothing a hand over his face. He looks exhausted. "Of course. I forgot we had those in here. Spare dish towels for the kitchen when we do our elder meal service."

"I'll help Gabe wash them when we're done. They'll be back in service by tomorrow."

"Hmm?" Mr. Beaudean glances over his shoulder, toward the church entry, and then straightens. "Don't worry about it, Del. We had to cancel this week's meal. I need to call Bobby and see if he can take on an extra day. I was just looking for a notepad to jot down a few notes."

I look at the desk and then back to Mr. Beaudean. Yeah, good luck with that. I keep the words to myself and skirt around his desk, clutching the towels.

Back in the sanctuary I thrust the towels at Gabe and flop down beside him. The trickle of water has slowed to a drip and Gabe is busy tossing wet towels into the waiting bucket. He presses a dry towel against the wall and wipes away the water.

I glance at my watch. Damn. "Sorry to mop and run, but I've got to get to the Gas & Gut. Ken will kill me if we open late."

Gabe nods, wedging a few more towels against the baseboard. "Sure. Thanks for the help."

"No problem. You coming by after my shift? We need to go over our notes on the miracles again."

"You helping me clean up the sanctuary tonight?" Gabe counters.

I narrow my eyes and rest my hands on my hips. "There better be chocolate chip cookies involved afterward."

"Of course," Gabe says with a wounded look. "I might even be able to rustle up some ice cream. There's a Godzilla marathon on tonight."

"Nice. I'll see you at six, then. But I'm bringing my notes. Miracles before radioactive lizards."

Gabe hides a grimace, but not quickly enough. So far, we haven't made much progress and he's getting tired of going over the same notes each night. So am I, but I'm not giving up.

CHAPTER TWENTY

Our Lady of the Wishing Well

Wednesday morning, I wake up an hour before my alarm goes off. Claire died a year ago today. I try to get out of bed but can't find the energy. Instead, I stare up at the ceiling. Above me a pattern of glow-in-the-dark stars is arranged like Capricorn, my birth sign. Mom put them there when I was eight. Two years later I helped her add a constellation for Claire's eighth birthday: Pisces. Claire's stars are gone. She took them down when she turned twelve and tacked up a picture of a cat peering down from a ceiling tile.

"Glow-in-the-dark stars are stupid," Claire had said. "Ceiling Cat will always be funny."

"Not laughing," I whisper, refusing to look at where the picture still hangs. A year. It's no time and a lifetime.

Downstairs, I ease open the liquor cabinet, pulling out a mostly empty bottle of brandy. The vodka bottles are still there, filled with water and air. Normally I wouldn't risk removing a bottle, just in case Mom checks. But today, more than any other, I'm going to need something to soften the edges of the world so I can sleep tonight. I creep back upstairs, slip the bottle under my bed, and then head noisily for the kitchen.

Emmet is already at the table, cradling a bowl of Cheerios and glaring at them like they've spelled out something insulting.

On the table in front of him is a huge vase of yellow roses with a little card tucked on the side. It's addressed to Mom but I swipe it and flip the thing over.

Our thoughts and prayers are with you on this difficult anniversary.

—Clemency School Board

As if flowers are going to make a difference. Claire preferred blue roses anyway. She said you had to work harder for them and that made them better.

I flick the card onto the table and it lands next to Emmet's clenched fist.

"Pretty," I say.

Emmet grunts and gets up from the table, dumping his Cheerios down the garbage disposal. "Let's go. There's a strategy session for the football team before class."

And life moves on. Emmet will throw himself into football, I'll go through the motions at school, and neither one of us will acknowledge the fact that everything fell apart a year ago today.

Gabe is waiting for me at school with a huge styrofoam coffee cup and a Milky Way bar. He hands them over without a word and pats my shoulder.

"I love you," I say fervently. The smells wafting from the coffee cup make me want to melt into a puddle on the school steps. A white chocolate mocha, proof that civilization is not a complete loss. It's exactly the rush of sugar and heat I need to chase away the awful feelings coiled in my stomach.

Gabe grins. "I knew that old cliché about girls and chocolate had to have something to it. A billion heart-shaped boxes can't be wrong." His smile slides away and he studies my expression. "How you holding up?"

"Fine. Just another day, right?"

Gabe winces. "Not exactly." I can see the confusion as he tries to figure out if I'm serious, if I've truly forgotten what today means.

I take pity on him—he did bring me sugar after all. "I'm not going to have a breakdown at school if that's what you're worried about."

"I'm worried about *you*, don't be stupid."

"I'll be okay, promise."

Gabe takes a deep breath and lets it out slowly. "If you want to talk or need a shoulder, I'm here."

I give him a curt nod and take a sip of coffee, the hot froth burning my tongue. It matches the burning in my chest.

"Is your family heading to the graveyard later?" Gabe asks.

"Not sure. If they are, I'm not going."

All I get for that is an exasperated sigh. Gabe hefts his backpack higher and bumps my shoulder with his. "Let's head inside."

Thank goodness he's letting it drop.

That first week after Claire died it was like someone had turned the sound off. Every one tiptoed around, whispered, and looked at me from the corners of their eyes. I expect today will be like that—a miniature time warp with the world bowing and bending around the black void

139

Claire left. She always could turn the world upside down and twist it however she wanted.

I was wrong. Today is worse. In a small town everyone knows everyone else's business and our memories are long. I will always be the girl with the dead sister. Everyone knows what today is. Everyone. The pitying looks are back. I prefer the angry glances I got right after the ABC segment, but they've completely disappeared. My teachers either avoid my eyes or, like Mrs. Morrison, pat my shoulder and murmur platitudes. I want to punch Mrs. M in the face. As a bonus, I'm pretty sure that would get me sent home. But I can't bring myself to do it. Yet.

By lunchtime I'm ready to snap and all it's going to take is one more whisper of Claire's name. Wendy springs up from her table when I enter the cafeteria. Oh hell no. I turn and bolt from the room, Wendy's shrill voice calling my name behind me.

I don't stop running until I'm out in the parking lot. If I had the keys, I'd take Rust Bucket and tear out of this place so fast. As it is, I have to stop by the time I reach the end of the parking lot because there's a burning pain in my side and I can barely catch my breath. I'm a walker, not a runner.

Bending, I rest my hands on my knees and suck in a breath. My backpack feels like it's loaded with bricks and it's sliding up my back thanks to my downward angle. There are no fences around the school, no bars across the parking lot. Nothing keeping us here, except the fact that every one of our teachers is on a first name basis with our parents. I don't care.

I walk down the road and the sun is hot on my face. The leaves rustle and sing. It's such a beautiful day. That feels like another betrayal. Today should be cloudy and gray. I don't know where I'm going. I just am.

I walk. Away from the school, away from the people. If I didn't know every corner of this town I could lose myself. But I'm always right here. The one thing I can't ever escape.

Everyone thinks I took Claire's death so hard because I loved her. And I did. But in the end I hated her too. I hated her so much. She ruined everything. She ruined our family. Her death erased me from the world for a long time because all anyone saw when they looked at me was my dead sister. I know she didn't have a choice. I'm not an idiot. It's not her fault she died. I hate myself for hating her. I hate God for hating both of us. Sometimes it feels like hate's all I have left inside.

I walk and walk and walk. There is no sense in the world. I think that's what I want more than anything, to understand why and how and what the hell comes next. One breath follows another. This whole year I've been searching for something. I'm not even sure what. My pictures pull me closer to it, my wall of proofs, but I still can't find it even now.

When I finally surface from my mental pity party, I'm over on Beecher Street, three miles from the school. Rather than houses, most of the homes on this street are single and double-wide trailers. They're decorated with wind chimes and white trellises, abandoned toys out front. It's a better class of trailer, the kind you have to save up for, the kind that probably isn't going to be moved elsewhere because it's practically fused to the foundation slab. Sometimes the trailers are nicer than the houses

141

in town—more time and effort put into keeping them pretty.

Case in point, the trailer in front of me, Melanie Teasedale's place. Mel is a clerk at the grocery store, stuck in Clemency taking care of her mom. Mel's in her thirties, and her mom isn't that old but early-onset dementia derailed both their lives a few years ago. Now Mel bags groceries, carries a shift at Maggio's on Fridays, and has to round up her mom every time Mrs. Teasedale wanders down Main Street in her nightie screaming at people to get off her damn lawn. For some reason Mrs. Teasedale is convinced the town square, with its wide gazebo, belongs to her.

You'd think with everything Mel has to do her place would be a wreck. Last thing she needs is yard work, right? That lawn is always perfectly trimmed, pretty boxwood bushes clipped and framing the tiny porch. Every spring she puts a fresh coat of wood stain on the tiny lawn-art wishing well and then crams it full of white flowers.

Now, with fall knocking on the door, the well cradles blazing yellow and orange mums. Like somebody shoved a sunset inside it.

Something is off about the well today though. I stare for a long moment, puzzling it out. There are dark splotches on the side, marring the wood. I take a few steps to the left to get a better angle.

"No freaking way."

An image of the Virgin Mary, hands extended at her sides and a halo radiating around her head, covers one side of the well. The image is blurry at the edges, dark and light swirling together to make a soft, dreamy picture, almost abstract. Her lips curve in a smile, as though she knows a secret.

CHAPTER TWENTY-ONE

Interview with a Grocery Clerk

I glance around, checking out the empty street before edging closer to the well and stepping onto Mrs. Teasedale's lawn. Beneath my sneakers the grass is spongy and soft, the ground still wet from being watered that morning. Despite that, I kneel down, wincing as damp seeps through my jeans at the knees.

I bend close to the well, tracing a finger over Mary's halo. The lines are darker at the edges; a myriad of browns blending together. The image seems to rise up from the wood, a natural part of it. I touch each line, tracing my fingers over the rough wood, searching for some hint of how the image was made. A tiny nick in the wood drags against my skin. There, at the bottom, a breath from the lines that form the roses resting on the tops of Mary's feet, is a thin scratch. A magnifying glass would come in handy right now.

My wet jeans press against my shins as I bend low, nose almost touching the wood. I squint, trying to see that one detail closer. It's a mirror of the line beside it. A guide. Someone lightly scratched the image in place using something sharp beforehand. Below, under the deeper brown, there's another small mark, like a tiny burn. My breath catches. As clues go, it's pretty crap, but it's the first real proof that the miracles aren't real. I pull back and fumble in my backpack for my camera, check there are still a few snapshots left, and then hold the camera as close to the image as I can without risking the focus. I'm prepared to admit, in this moment only, that a Polaroid isn't the perfect photo in every instance. I could use a high-res digital camera in addition to that magnifying glass.

I snap the picture and wait as the camera spits out its tiny white-framed square. It's only as I'm waiting for the picture to finish developing that it occurs to me I might be stalking Mel's lawn art for nothing. She could have paid someone to come decorate her wishing well. No implied miracles at all.

The photo is marginally helpful; you can sorta make out the scratched line against the wood grain. My extreme close-up of Mary's feet looks like an abstract painting. I step back and snap another picture, this one of the entire image. If this is more than just a home improvement project, I want plenty of photographic evidence.

I look up and down the street again. It's still quiet. Peaceful. We're far enough from Main Street that you can't hear the traffic, and no out-of-towners are tramping around. Such a contrast to the noise and rush of school. To the tension at home. I think of Claire and the graveyard, of Emmet and his long silences. I think of Mom, hiding at work, and Dad hiding in another state.

The burning is back in my chest and I focus on the wishing well instead. I need this mystery. These miracles are fake. I know it and I'm going to prove it. Whether this town likes it or not. Whether it costs me my job. Screw Mayor Thompson. This could be the clue Gabe and I need to crack the case. I just have to figure out how.

I debate knocking on Mel's door to ask about the wishing well. Better not. Mrs. Teasedale might brain me with a frying pan. Besides, one-ish on a Wednesday? Mel's at the grocery for sure. My stomach growls, reminding me I ran out during lunch hour and all I've had today is a candy bar and some coffee. The sugar crash is probably contributing to my bad mood.

I search my pockets, finding a crumpled five-dollar bill. The remains of my last paycheck. But it's enough to get a sandwich and soda from the grocery deli. And the perfect excuse for chatting up Mel. Maybe she's the miracle mastermind and all of the other miracles were leading up to this one, conveniently sitting in her front yard.

When I walk into Bryer's Grocery fifteen minutes later, the place is hopping. There are at least twenty people milling around that I can see, and five already standing in line at the lone cash register. Mel is swiping items across the scanner and having a cheerful one-sided conversation with a woman in a purple jogging suit who keeps checking her watch.

"I don't understand how you can be out of milk," the woman interrupts.

Mel gives a small shrug. "It's been busy."

Understatement of the year. I eye the other customers and re-evaluate my lunch plans. The damn out-of-towners are like locusts, gobbling up everything in their path.

I turn my attention back to Mel. Her brown hair is bleached light blonde, the roots dark. She's stuck between skinny and overweight, with a solid body frame that could never be called anything except big-boned.

Mel catches sight of me and her eyes widen, darting to the clock above the employee break room door. "Did something happen at the school?" she asks, suddenly ignoring the customer in front of her.

The woman taps the counter. "Excuse me? I'd appreciate if you could finish checking me out, please."

I give Mel a reassuring smile and stop at the end of the lane. I begin bagging groceries and that shuts the snotty woman up. Apparently if I work for the privilege, I'm allowed to talk to Mel.

"I couldn't take the cafeteria food," I say. Mel attended Shrenk High years ago. She knows it's a closed campus and I'm not supposed to be here.

She frowns for a moment but then her expression melts into a compassionate grimace. "Tough day today? I'm sure Principal Candlewhite would understand if you need to take the day off and spend it with your family."

She scans the last item and gives the woman her total in an extra cheerful voice, shifting her focus for a moment.

Great. Even the grocery clerk has a mental calendar with a big red star slapped on today. Maybe next year they'll make it a town-wide holiday honoring Saint Claire.

I hand two sacks of groceries to jogging suit lady and she gives me a blank look. "Aren't you going to walk them out to my car?"

"It's self serve, lady. Grab a cart if they're too heavy."

"Delaney!" Mel says in a quiet voice, then turns to the woman. "I'm sorry, ma'am, we don't have any extra clerks right now."

The woman hmphs and storms off with her groceries. There's a guy in line next and he nudges his bag of potato chips toward the scanner meaningfully. Mel bites her lip and fumbles the bag across the scanner.

"I'm sorry, Del. I can't talk right now."

"I understand," I say. Maybe a new tactic is called for. I move to the deli counter and discover there are still a few sandwich supplies left. Blake, one of Bryer's other perennial employees, throws a sandwich together for me and passes it over without comment. I appreciate his lack of conversational skill. He's in his late twenties, gaunt and pallid with a hoop earring in one ear. A scrub of reddish-brown hair clings to his chin but his head is completely bald. He looks like Mr. Clean's younger, skinnier brother.

"Thanks," I say. Blake merely nods. Maybe he's taken a vow of silence. Or maybe years of working with Mel and her near-constant chatter have seized up his vocal cords.

I get in line to pay for my sandwich and grab an IBC root beer as well. When I finally get to the register, there's no one in line behind me, thank goodness. This is my chance.

"I passed by your place earlier," I say.

Mel tenses. "Was Mom out in the yard again?"

"No, but I—uh—like what you've done with the wishing well." I try to look casual but every cell in my body is on high alert.

"The new mums are gorgeous, aren't they? I drove all the way to Ashby for them." Mel beams, taking my money and handing back change.

"No, I mean the decorative panel you added to the front."

Mel frowns. "It's a wooden well, there aren't any decorations. Other than my flowers, of course."

"There's definitely something on there now," I say. "An image."

Mel's frown morphs into a little *oh* of surprise and her eyes widen. "Did someone deface my well?" She throws

147

a look at the handful of people still browsing the aisles closest to us and lowers her voice to a whisper. "Do you think it was gangs?"

"I think gangs normally use spray paint, and it definitely wasn't." I suppress a laugh. Yeah, roving gang bangers drove all the way from the city to graffiti our town. Not.

Mel chews her bottom lip. "Is it bad? Something obscene? Maybe I should call the police station."

I hold up a hand, placating. We only have three cops for the entire county and at least one of them is on permanent duty outside the McDonald's these days. If the other two rush to Mel's looking for phantom gangs, I'll probably get a ticket for inciting a false report. "It's fine. It's a religious symbol, not a gang sign."

Mel's eyes widen. Suddenly she breaks into a huge grin. "It's another miracle!"

It's a sign of how crazy things have gotten that she's made the leap from graffiti to miracle in mere seconds. And unless Mel has insane acting skills she's never displayed before, I'm pretty sure she didn't know about Wishing Well Mary until I told her. Damn.

I mentally kick myself. I could have ripped the panel off the well and had the latest miracle to study for as long as I need to figure out who's dicking with our town. Now it's way too late for that. A few of the people in the store are already looking at Mel curiously.

Mel whirls and faces Blake. "Did you hear?" Her face is shining and there are tears in her eyes. Her hands knot together and then release over and over. She looks like she might bounce right out of her shoes at any moment. "A real, live miracle on my front lawn. Maybe God has healed my mom!" She glances at the clock again and bites

148

her lip. "I have to go, Blake. You understand, right? I have to check."

He nods, frowning in confusion. Mel yanks off her grocery apron and bolts for the door. I can see at least one guy pulling out his cell phone and I hightail it out of there. The latest miracle is about to become big news.

CHAPTER TWENTY-TWO

The Day the Networks Came to Town

After leaving the grocery store, I wander for a while, trying to kill time. No way I'm heading back to school. When I finally get home, Gabe is waiting for me, perched by my front door, back pressed into the red brick of the house and head bent over the Nintendo DS he's clutching. He thumbs feverishly at the controls. My shadow stretches across Gabe and he looks up, squinting.

"Figured you'd have to come home eventually," he says. He pushes to his feet and tucks the DS into his backpack.

"I needed some air. And you're never going to guess what I found."

I step past Gabe and unlock the front door, motioning him inside. He squeezes past me, making my stomach clench at the brush of his body against mine. In a different world, if I was a different person, maybe I'd be brave enough to tell him how I feel.

Upstairs something thumps to the floor and we both look up. I glance at my watch. Mom should still be sleeping; she won't start getting ready for her shift for another couple of hours.

"Be right back," I tell Gabe and dash upstairs.

I pause outside Mom's room, hand raised to knock. The sound of someone crying stops me. I let my hand drop to my side and press my forehead against the door, listening. A good person would go inside and comfort her. A good person would forgive her for being so caught up in her grief that she doesn't have time for anything else.

I turn and walk away.

"Everything okay?" Gabe asks when I enter the kitchen.

I shrug and pop some frozen pizza bites into the microwave, zapping the hell out of them. When Gabe's stuffed a bunch in his mouth, I tell him about the wishing well. He chokes.

I scramble up and get him a glass of water before he turns blue from lack of oxygen.

When he can breathe again he glares. "Are you trying to kill me? Don't spring that stuff when I'm eating!"

"Sorry," I mutter. I wait a long second, giving him a chance to gulp down some more water. "I got some pictures."

Gabe nods. "Excellent, let's have a look."

He studies them for a long time and I wait impatiently before finally blurting, "You see it, don't you?"

When he doesn't immediately respond with "Yes! Of course. You've solved it all, you genius!" I lean over and move the detail shot in front of the other Polaroid.

Gabe tilts his head to the side and wrinkles his nose. "It's a blurry photo. Not sure what I'm supposed to be getting out of this."

I drag a finger over the faint gouge mark by Mary's feet. "Look! Someone traced the image first and then somehow painted it. That tool mark proves the miracles are a fake."

Gabe lifts the picture and squints, then shakes his head. "Looks like part of the wood grain."

I throw my hands up. "Grab a magnifying glass and let's go over there now. I'll prove it."

"Where am I supposed to dig up a magnifying glass?"

I glare at Gabe, convinced he's being deliberately difficult, and then inspiration strikes. I hold up a finger. "Give me a minute."

I dash to my bedroom and rifle through my nightstand drawer. Back in the kitchen, I brandish the tiny figure at Gabe.

Gabe's wariness dissolves as he starts laughing. "Garfield? Seriously? We're going to solve the great miracle mystery with a toy Garfield?"

"Shut up," I mutter, holding the plastic toy tighter. I yank on Garfield's tail and part of his back slides out, revealing a magnifying glass panel. "I got him at McDonald's when I was like five. He has sentimental value. *And* he magnifies things."

Gabe takes Garfield when I hold him out, but he's still laughing too hard to talk. Okay, I know my mini Garfield is ridiculous but it's the best I can do on short notice. Gabe's laughter is starting to get annoying. He gets up and takes a package of powdered doughnuts off the microwave top, using the magnifying glass to read the tiny print on the label.

"This might work," Gabe says, voice hoarse. He slides Garfield closed and shakes his head. "Detectives everywhere are hanging their heads in shame for us."

Taking Garfield back, I sniff, narrowing my eyes. "Do you want to go see the well or not?"

Gabe tries his best to look solemn, but I can tell he's still hiding a grin. "Sure."

We never make it to Melanie Teasedale's place. There's a fleet of news vans blocking every side street leading into her neighborhood and a crowd of people thick enough for the Macy's Thanksgiving Day Parade.

Gabe parks his car five blocks over and we thread our way through the crowds. We stop behind a knot of people, unable to move any closer. Everyone is talking and it sounds like a giant engine rumbling.

Gabe leans close and yells in my ear, "This place is a zoo. Is that a CNN truck?"

I crane my head, trying to distinguish one news van from the other. They clog the narrow streets like an artery blockage, tight packed and out of place. I finally spot the van Gabe means and my eyes widen. It is CNN. I look more closely at the other vans. A couple are local stations from Ashby, but there's one van from Dallas and I spot a Houston station as well. There's a black car with an AP logo plastered on the side. A lanky guy in ratty jeans and a T-shirt gets out, holding a camera as big as my head.

Gabe and I linger for an hour and the crowd gets bigger and bigger. At one point Officer Crowley, one of the local cops, raises a bullhorn and asks the crowd to disperse, warning us that we're trampling private property and blocking homes. No one moves. Mel's neighbors have dragged lawn chairs in front of their houses and one old lady, Mrs. Renley, is gleefully munching on popcorn as she ogles the press vans and the crowd.

It's impossible to hear any of the news anchors from where we're standing. After someone jabs an elbow in my back for the third time and I've had my foot stomped yet again, I squeeze Gabe's arm, saying, "This is stupid. Let's grab a couch at your place and find a news station. We might actually learn something."

Gabe nods, eying Melanie's roof in the distance. After we've fought our way back to the car, Gabe leans over and gives me a quick hug. "Sorry Garfield has to miss his shining moment."

I shove him away, laughing. Unfortunately, Gabe's car is now gridlocked by other vehicles, so we leave it parked and walk back to his place. We check every single lawn ornament along the way, searching for rogue miracles. This time, if we find one, I'm taking the thing and asking questions later.

CHAPTER TWENTY-THREE

Waiting for a Miracle

Gabe's house is quiet. Reverend Beaudean spends late hours working at the church or visiting with various congregants. Sometimes he uses the church van if Gabe's got the Taurus. All of that means Gabe has lots of time to himself and we don't have any competition for the TV tonight.

We sit side by side on his couch, flipping between news stations. CNN, predictably, airs their story first. A shot of the Clemency welcome sign, flanked by another picture of Baby Cheesus, fills the screen behind the news anchor. The two images fade to black for a moment and then there's an image of Mel's front yard with the words MIRACLES IN MIDDLE AMERICA hovering in giant red teletype above.

"Isn't Kansas middle America?" I ask. "We're south. Southwest if you want to get technical."

"News stations like alliteration," Gabe says. "Quiet down, they're starting."

"Tonight we bring you a special story right out of the Heartland of America. Many are questioning whether God's hand is at work in a tiny Texas town as miracle after miracle appears."

The bubbly news anchor smiles at the camera and runs through the story of Baby Cheesus being found and the image appearing on the McDonald's drive-through window. A moment later the screen cuts to a live video feed from Mel's front yard. Mel stands beside the well, smoothing her hands down the sides of her pants and looking terrified by the cameras.

Beside Mel, a man with slicked-back hair and a dimple in his chin smiles confidently and half turns to face the camera. "Wyatt Owens here on location in Clemency, Texas. I'm speaking with Melanie Teasedale. Miss Teasedale, please tell me about this remarkable well and the impact it is already having on your life."

Mel glances at the house behind her and then back at the reporter. "We feel so blessed to have been visited by God and given one of his miracles."

Before she can continue, the front door of the house bangs open and Mrs. Teasedale charges out in her pink floral nightgown, white hair frizzed around her head like Einstein and a frying pan clutched in both hands. The old lady pauses for a moment, narrowing her eyes at the reporter and Mel before raising her pan and screaming, "Get off my lawn! Get! Get!"

Mel's face turns red. She hurries to put herself between her mother and the reporter. "Mom! Go back in the house. Everything is fine."

"Don't you talk back to me!" Mrs. Teasedale screams. "Out here carrying on with boys, Melanie. Trampling my daisies! When your father gets home, he'll take a strap to you."

The old woman reaches Mel and the reporter and takes a shaky swing with her pan. Mel grabs her mother's arm and wrestles the pan away, crying now. The reporter dances back, one hand pressed to his ear, holding his earpiece in place and sputtering.

Mrs. Teasedale's eyes are narrowed with spite and flecks of spit cling to the corners of her mouth. "Get off my lawn! You get on out of here. Go on, get!" Gabe flips the TV off and we sit frozen. Our smiles and laughter sucked into the now blank screen.

"That was awful." I dig my fingers into the edge of the couch cushion. "Poor Mel."

Gabe nods, setting down the TV remote as though it's a stick of dynamite. "They used to come to Holy Cross every Sunday, but they've missed a couple weeks. Dad's been by twice but he didn't say anything about Mrs. Teasedale losing her mind."

I stare at the dark TV screen, unable to forget Mel's tears and her mother's screaming. "You should have seen Mel at the store today. She really thought God might have cured her mom. I guess she didn't get the miracle she was expecting."

"That's not fair," Gabe mutters. "Maybe he gave her the miracle she needed. We don't know how things will turn out with that well."

"I'm sure that's a huge comfort right now," I snap.

"Del," Gabe begins, but I cut him off.

"No, you want to prove the miracles are real? Fine. Show me a shred of evidence. Tell me how that well has done anything to make Mel's life better."

"She only found it a few hours ago." Gabe throws up his hands. "Not everything happens right away."

"What about Baby Cheesus? It's been weeks since Andy found it. That should be long enough for you. What good has that cheese wheel done? Or McJesus? A bunch of questionable healings, a crush of idiot people invading our town. There's no evidence any of the miracles are real."

"There's no evidence they aren't," Gabe counters. "I thought that's what we were doing. Or are you finally willing to admit you've got a personal agenda for all of this? You think if you prove the miracles aren't real you can prove God isn't real either?"

The words cut through me, sharp as shards of glass. Nausea rolls in a slow burn up my throat. "That isn't the point," I whisper. Even though it partially is. It's all so complicated. Part of me doesn't want to believe in God anymore. The larger part, though, needs God to be real if only so I can blame him for Claire's death. Someone has to be responsible. It can't be Claire and it can't be me. Please, please, it can't be me.

Gabe softens, reaching out to brush my cheek. I flinch away and he drops his arm.

I've never been able to hide from Gabe. That scares me. There are dark places inside I don't ever want him to see, things I've done that I can't ever share.

"Please, Del." Gabe's look is pleading. "I don't know what to say to help you." He makes a frustrated noise. "My dad would know what to do."

"I doubt it." My voice is thick and waterlogged. I get up from the couch and touch Gabe's shoulder. "I'm gonna head home. You don't have to help me with the miracles, I'll figure out who's doing this on my own."

The words burn my lips as I say them. But Gabe's a preacher's kid and that's never gonna change. He'll always be on the side of miracles and I'll always be hanging with the skeptics. I should've known asking him to help me investigate was a terrible idea.

Gabe scrambles up, softness dropping away in a heartbeat. "I said I'd help. Don't shut me out of this too."

"What's that supposed to mean?" I'm doing the noble thing, walking away. He should just let me.

"I'm tired of you shoving me to the edges of your life. You won't talk to me, not about anything important. Every time I bring up Claire or your family, you shut down, give me some snarky answer and move on. Every time things get tough, you run away." He meets my eyes and won't look away. "So I'm not ready to picket the miracles. That doesn't mean I'm not trying to help. I'm here. I'm the one who's been writing down lists and helping you come up with theories."

"You don't actually want to do any of that though. I'm sorry I dragged you into this." My dramatic speech is ruined by the fact my voice is shaking but I hold my ground.

Gabe throws his hands up in the air and storms back to the couch. "You asked me to help."

"It was a mistake." Words are spilling from my mouth and they won't be dragged back no matter how hard I try.

"Fine. Walk out. Go prove everyone is wrong and the mighty Del, martyr extraordinaire, is right."

"What do you want from me?" I scream. The sound shocks us both and we freeze, eyes wide.

"You," Gabe whispers. I'm holding my breath, poised at the edge of something. "You're my best friend. Don't walk out on me too."

There is an entire world of meaning in those last words. Don't walk out on him like I've walked out on my family, my sister's memory, my classes, my sometimes-friends at school. Don't walk out on Gabe like his mom, his always-busy-with-the-church dad. I crumple under the weight of those words.

"I'm sorry." My voice is raw and low, blood dripping from the edges. "I don't know what else to do."

"Let me help you," Gabe pleads.

"Proving it's all a hoax?" I want to laugh, throw the words in his face, make him hurt as much as I do, but he already does. I can see it in the way his lips press together, the way he stands as though waiting for a wrecking ball to smack into him.

"Prove something. Whichever way it goes. But together, okay. We do it together or not at all."

He holds out his pinky toward me and a broken laugh slips past my lips. "Aren't we a little old for pinky swears?"

"You're never too old for pinky swears." Gabe's voice is solemn, but there's something fragile about his expression. If I turn around and leave his hand hanging in the air, some vital part of our friendship will shatter and I won't be able to fit the pieces together again.

I take one step forward, and then another, until we're close enough that the tips of our shoes touch. I hook my pinky with his and squeeze tight.

"Together," I say and Gabe squeezes back.

Chapter Twenty-Four

Ninja Reconnaissance

D o you want to go over our notes again?" Gabe asks.

I shake my head. We're back on the couch, both trying to act like we weren't arguing a few minutes ago. Talking about the investigation is easier. Gabe's suggestion is a good one, but our notes haven't changed and so far, they haven't gotten us anywhere. We have plenty of suspects, plenty of motives, but no proof and no leads. Which leaves the miracles themselves.

Maybe we need to start at the beginning and look at each miracle again. Study them in person. Melanie's front lawn will still be packed and Baby Cheesus is on lockdown at St. Andrew's. I doubt Gabe's willingness to help me extends to breaking and entering.

"We should take a closer look at McJesus," I say. "It's on display at the McDonalds and I need better pictures anyway."

Gabe nods a little too quickly, but I pretend not to notice. "Makes sense. Let me change my shirt and then we'll head out."

There are wet patches on his T-shirt from where I pressed my face against his chest when we hugged after our pinky swear. I nod and mumble an assent.

He heads for his bedroom and I trail behind, stopping just inside his door. Gabe snags a dark blue T-shirt from his closet and then shrugs off the old one. He doesn't have washboard abs but his stomach's flat and taut with a dusting of hair below his belly button. I glance away, cheeks flushing. It's not like I haven't seen him in swim trunks a hundred times, but back then I wasn't battling an insane crush.

I focus on the wall closest to me. Unlike the chaotic flood of pictures covering my walls, Gabe's decorations are sparse, wide expanses of plain white visible. A Death Star blueprint hangs over his desk and there's a promo poster for one of those cringe-worthy country bands he listens to taped beside his door. His old Ninja Turtles lamp still sits on the bedside table, a pile of school books stacked beside it. The blankets stretched across Gabe's bed are mismatched—one blue, one red, a white sheet underneath.

We've never spent much time in Gabe's room, preferring to run wild outside or raid my parents' kitchen. I have the urge to grab a bucket of paint and attack his walls, to add a bit more life to the place.

"No," Gabe says, walking across the room and stopping beside me.

"I didn't do anything." I give him the side-eye.

"You're staring at my walls and you've got the same expression as that time you wanted to play barber and I wound up having to shave my head." Gabe scowls, but I can see the smile hiding underneath.

I reach up, rubbing the short, tight curls covering his head. "You were cute bald. I think I did you a favor."

Gabe ducks away and shakes his head. "Whatever you're planning for my room, don't. I like it the way it is now. It's relaxing."

"It's boring." I step around Gabe and run a hand over the bare wall. "I could donate a few pictures."

162

"Not a chance."

I frown, twisting to glance over my shoulder at Gabe. My hip bumps his desk and knocks a small wooden box loose, sending it crashing to the floor. Dozens of envelopes spill out—most are white but there are a few blues and greens mixed in.

"Sorry!" I crouch down, snatching at envelopes and trying to make a neat pile.

Gabe joins me and it's like a game of 52-Card Pickup with very large, awkwardly shaped cards. Each envelope has a date handwritten on the back flap and none of them have stamps or an address.

I look up at Gabe when I find an envelope dated last week. "You still write her?"

His cheeks flush and he holds out a hand for the envelope. "Yeah. Sometimes."

"She doesn't deserve it." I lay the envelope in his hand, wanting to burn the sad pile of letters.

"She's still my mom," Gabe says.

I don't have an answer for that. Gabe started writing Lila letters and making cards for her the first Christmas after she ran off. I thought he'd stopped years ago. What's the point? She's never coming back.

For the first time since my dad got in his car and headed for Montana, I'm grateful for his random five-minute phone calls. He's still a jerk for leaving us, but he's making more of an effort to stay in touch than Lila ever has.

We finish gathering the envelopes in silence, not looking at each other. When we're done, Gabe places the box back on his desk and I try to think of something to break the tension. My eyes linger on the bare wall in front of us.

Sudden inspiration strikes and I tap a finger against the wall. "We could use this as a pin board—like on one of those cop shows you're always watching. We pin up pictures of all the miracles, write our notes and suspect list. We can add little arrows connecting things."

"You are not drawing on my walls." Gabe grabs my shoulders and eases me away from his wall, not letting go until I'm standing in the middle of his room.

"It's a great idea! You have all this space."

"I like my space. I like my plain white walls." Gabe sighs and drops into his desk chair, resting an elbow on the desktop.

"What if I hang paper instead, then we can take it down when we're done," I say. "Or move it to my place." Gabe still looks skeptical and I make puppy dog eyes at him. "Please?"

After another dramatic sigh he drags a hand over his face and nods. "Fine. But only on paper."

"Yes!" I punch the air in triumph. "Go get me a stack of printer paper and some clear tape—it's crafty time."

"This is your idea, grab your own supplies," Gabe grumbles, but he gets up and heads for the door.

I grin at him. "You know you love me."

Gabe hesitates a moment, shoulder brushing mine as he stops beside me. I look up, smile sliding away. I feel like I swallowed a baseball, voice trapped in my throat. Then Gabe shoves me and sprints out of the room, cackling.

I stagger, catch my balance, and yell after him, "Just for that, you get to do all the taping!"

After assembling our makeshift board—ten pages wide and six pages high—we hang it on the wall and then head out.

164

"We just need a couple good pictures of the drive-through window so we can add them to the board," I tell Gabe.

"I think calling it a board is a bit of a stretch." Gabe locks his front door behind him and then lopes over to his car.

"We agreed to take this seriously. Don't insult my new idea board." I shake a finger at Gabe as I slide into the passenger seat.

"I am humoring a clearly insane girl, only because of our long and baffling friendship."

The word "baffling" makes me wince. Does Gabe regret our friendship? I run my fingers over the edge of my seat, anchoring myself here and now.

"I was only kidding about you being insane," Gabe says. "Mostly." His voice is falsely cheerful and I catch him shooting me sideways looks as he drives.

"Ha ha. Don't forget who's running this mission, buddy." I match his tone of voice, back to pretending nothing is wrong.

McDonald's is packed. No surprise there. In the parking lot I spot a news van, the Houston NBC affiliate, but otherwise it looks reporter free. There's a sign taped to each of the restaurant doors, black Sharpie on baby blue paper: "Miracle Special: Two McFish sandwiches and large fries for $5." Ew. Gabe grimaces as well, but I have a feeling it's the "Miracle Special" bit and not the fish sandwiches upsetting him.

"That is not what Jesus meant when he multiplied the fish and the bread," Gabe mutters.

"But it's double the deep-fried goodness," I tease.

Gabe shudders. "Let's get in there and get the pictures. No ordering the special."

Inside, I spot the news people right away, a well-dressed guy in a suit far too nice for Clemency and a couple other people hovering near him like small moons in orbit. They're all too tanned and, although the reporter's support crew aren't dressed as nicely, there's still something that clearly marks them as out-of-towners. Maybe it's the way they move, in quick jerky spasms. No one in Clemency moves fast unless something's on fire.

In the middle of the restaurant, the drive-through window panel with McJesus hangs suspended from the ceiling by two thin chains. Below it, there's a four-foot square roped off, the edge of each corner marked by a bright orange traffic cone with caution tape stretching between them. Very classy. But I suppose Mr. Henderson doesn't want anyone getting fingerprints on his holy window.

I was hoping to get a couple close-up shots but it looks like that's going to be difficult.

"Well?" Gabe prompts. He's standing, head cocked and hands loose at his sides.

I sigh and pull out the camera. Its solid bulk in my hands feels good, relaxing me.

I step as close to the window as I can get, my knees brushing the caution tape. After checking the little number counter on the back of my camera to make sure I still have film left—nine shots to go—I press my eye to the viewfinder and line up the shot. A moment later a picture slides from the front of the camera and I hand it to Gabe. Working quickly, I take one more and then step to the back of the window and snap another picture.

Something catches my eye. "Gabe, come check this out."

"Del, what are you up to?" a voice booms from the front of the store and I jump, glancing up to see that most of the restaurant patrons are staring at Gabe and me. The looks range from curious to downright hostile. The restaurant's manager, Mr. Henderson, stands by the cash register and his eyes dart from the reporter in front of him back to me. I can practically see the gears in his head turning, panic ratcheting up. Del + reporter = disaster.

I wave and flash him a broad smile, trying to look innocent and unthreatening. I hold up one of the Polaroids. "Getting some pictures for my wall."

Mr. Henderson tenses and looks ready to argue but just then the reporter in front of him checks his watch and Mr. H huffs out a breath. "Don't get too close. That tape is there to protect McJesus."

I nod. "Sure thing."

As soon as Mr. Henderson turns back to the reporter, I drag Gabe over to look at the back of the window. "See?" I demand, pointing.

Gabe squints and shakes his head. "What am I looking for?"

"There, in the bottom corner. You can't see it from the front, but doesn't that look like a brush stroke? From a paintbrush?"

Gabe leans forward as far as he can. "Maybe. It's hard to tell."

"I need a better picture." I press the camera closer against my body. Mr. Henderson is still chatting away at the counter. A couple wanders up on the other side of McJesus, looking at the front of the window. This is our chance. I glance around the restaurant; it's crowded and I'm still getting a few dirty looks but we're never going to have a better chance.

I shove Gabe to the left. "Stand there and don't move."

Gabe splutters but I step over the tape and hold the camera close to the window. I snap a picture as Mr. Henderson looks up and notices me.

"I said don't cross the tape, Del!"

I jump back over, grab Gabe's hand, and begin tugging him toward the front door. "Sorry, sir. I couldn't resist."

We bolt, Gabe running beside me as we shove through the front doors.

Safe in the car, Gabe twists to glare at me. "You know he's going to call my dad, right?"

"Totally worth it. We got the pictures we needed." I hold up the four Polaroids, including the all-important close-up.

Chapter Twenty-Five

Mixed Signals

We head to my house to pick up the other pictures. Gabe flips on the radio, blasting Alabama so loud my ears are about to start bleeding. He's punishing me for getting him in trouble. Scratch that—potentially getting him in trouble. Because it's not for sure Mr. Henderson will call his dad. And seriously, what's the worst Mr. Beaudean would do? Ground Gabe? That's happened like twice in the entire time I've known him and both times he just lost video game privileges for a week. Okay, so both times were technically my fault but who's keeping track?

I remain silent, though. Now is not the time for inspired logic. Let Gabe torture my eardrums—he'll get over our little adventure faster.

When we pull up in front of my house, Gabe cuts the engine and twists to face me.

"You are pure trouble sometimes." His voice is exasperated. A good sign.

"You'd be bored without me." I give him a small smile.

Gabe slumps back in his seat, shaking his head. "Maybe."

A moment later, we slip inside my house. Mom is at work, as usual. I pause in the entry hall and listen for Emmet. The house is dead quiet. Maybe Emmet's on a date. Best not to think about my brother playing tonsil hockey; I might throw up.

"We've got the place to ourselves." I fling my hands out as though welcoming Gabe to Buckingham Palace.

"Remind me again why we're not setting up our idea board here?"

"You've got more space." Upstairs, we walk down the hall to my room and I turn on the light, gesturing to my walls.

Gabe winces dramatically and then squints at the area over my dresser. "I think you missed a spot; I can see some wall. Run out of film again?"

"Shut up. The film packs might be insanely expensive, but I like my pictures. It's like sitting in a room with a million little windows."

Gabe shakes his head but walks over and flops onto my bed, shoes and all. He looks ridiculous against the pink duvet. It was Claire's, and despite being utterly hideous, it's one of the few reminders that Claire once shared this room with me.

"Feet off," I tell Gabe, slapping the tops of his sneakers.

He grumbles but shifts to dangle his feet off the side of my bed.

"So, where are the other pictures?" he asks.

I grab a pile of Polaroids from the dresser top and begin flipping through. "I haven't hung them up yet." Some have titles scrawled on the bottom, already destined for my proofs wall. Some are merely random snapshots that I can use to fill up space. Most, though, have something to do with the miracles.

The front door bangs open, making me jump.

"Anyone home?" Emmet's voice booms down the hall. There's a muffled giggle. Holy shit. He's snuck a girl into the house. Who?

"I'm sure my sister's home," Emmet says, sounding strained.

Gabe levers himself into a sitting position and raises his eyebrows at me.

"This is why we can't use my house," I hiss.

"We're in here," Gabe calls out, grinning at me.

I glare back.

There's a hesitation, another giggle, and then Emmet is standing in my doorway looking between me and Gabe. He seems oddly relieved.

I'll bet he thought I was making out with a boy up here. Clearly he's not worried about Gabe feeling me up. That is so typically Emmet. So typically Clemency. Because Gabe and I have been friends since before we developed acne and hormones, everyone assumes there's no way we'd ever be anything other than friends. It's annoying.

I rest both hands on my hips and give Emmet my best death stare. Sadly, he's immune. Hovering in the hallway behind Emmet, Anna Jankowski gives me a little wave. What is one of Wendy's clones doing in my house? Anna sidles up to Emmet and slips her arm through his. She's wearing a baby-pink top so tight it looks like she's raided her kid sister's closet.

Emmet glances down at Anna, and I swear sweat breaks out on his forehead. I bet he can see right down the front of that top. Guess he's moved on from his mystery girl of a few weeks ago. Then again, Emmet's not exactly a one-girl kinda guy and Anna is rubbing up against him like a cat in heat.

Emmet's phone rings and he untangles Anna from his arm and snatches the cell from his pocket. He checks the display, but instead of answering, he hits a button to refuse the call before slipping the phone back into his pocket.

"Who's that?" Anna asks with a dramatic pout.

"No one," Emmet mumbles.

I bet it was another girl calling. My brother the player, ladies and gentlemen. I finally notice the I SAW CHEESUS button Emmet's sporting on his grungy white T-shirt. "You've got to be kidding me."

Emmet scowls. "What?"

"Why are you wearing one of Ken's stupid buttons?"

Anna breaks into a smile. "Isn't it cute? All the players and cheerleaders are wearing them to show our support for Clemency and St. Andrew's."

I look pointedly at Anna's button free top. "*All* the cheerleaders?"

She flushes and latches onto Emmet's arm again. "This shirt is a Julie B. Taylor original. It was not cheap. I can't put holes in it!"

Emmet's phone rings again and before he can make a move, Anna reaches into his pocket and pulls it free. I think she might have just groped my brother as well. Ew. I need to Lysol my eyes.

"Don't," Emmet says, but it's too late. Anna has flipped open the phone and answers with a throaty, "Emmet's busy right now, can I help you?"

Emmet goes dead white. He's so busted. I can't help smirking as I watch him squirm.

"Oh," Anna says, stiffening. Her voice loses the sex kitten vibe and she switches back to down-home cheer-leader. "I'm his girlfriend, Anna."

Emmet looks like he's going to strangle her. While I'm sure he's earned whatever mess he's in right now, I don't want my brother to go to jail. I take a step forward, angling toward Anna. If I tackle Emmet it'll be like hitting a brick wall—better to aim for the smaller target.

172

Anna, meanwhile, is still busy on the phone. "Hang on, I'll get him for y—" She pulls the phone away from her ear and glares at it. "That was rude. He just hung up on me."

She flips the phone shut and hands it back to Emmet. He snatches it away from her, glaring.

"We aren't dating," Emmet snarls.

Anna pouts. "So what was tonight all about? You asked me over just for sex?"

This conversation has officially moved from awkward to "get me the hell out of here now" territory. I switch direction and move back to Gabe, shoving the Polaroids into his hands. He nods, knowing what I want because clearly he wants out of here just as much.

"We're gonna get going," Gabe says. He tucks the Polaroids into his backpack and gets up from the bed.

Emmet doesn't spare us a look, still focused on Anna. "I didn't ask you over. You ambushed me in the parking lot after practice and said we needed to talk about Friday's pep rally."

"You drove me here!" Anna stamps her foot.

They're blocking the doorway and neither one of them looks like they're moving any time soon. I sincerely regret not keeping rope in my room so I can bust out my window and rappel down the side wall.

"Hey," I try, raising my voice. "I'm sorry, but Gabe and I need to go. Any chance you can move this to the kitchen? Maybe the driveway? Canada if possible?"

Emmet turns his glare on me. "Not now, Del!"

"Whoa, whatever's going on, it's not her fault," Gabe snaps. "Chill out."

Emmet grinds his teeth and narrows his eyes at Gabe. He looks like an enraged bull. I step between my brother and my best friend, holding my hands up.

"Guys, seriously." I switch my gaze to Anna, "Why don't Gabe and I take you home. You and Emmet can talk things out tomorrow."

Anna's lips quiver and she gives a quick nod, keeping tear-filled eyes on Emmet. "I can't believe you're acting this way, after everything we've shared."

Emmet curses and storms downstairs.

I snatch my bag and Gabe and I herd Anna out of the hall and down to his car.

Everything they've shared? Has Emmet been hooking up with Anna for a while now? How did I miss that? Thanks to several disturbing mental images that pop into my head, I need to Lysol my brain in addition to my eyes.

When we're in Gabe's car, Anna begins to sob quietly. She's pretty even now, with red-rimmed eyes and chest heaving. I can't help hating her, especially when I catch Gabe giving her concerned, sympathetic looks.

I turn away and catch sight of Emmet sitting behind the wheel inside Rust Bucket. He's on the phone, clearly arguing with someone, gesturing wildly even though whoever is on the other side of that call can't see him. Suddenly Emmet rips the phone away from his ear and flings it at the windshield. I've never seen my brother out of control. It's terrifying. A moment later, Rust Bucket peels away from the curb and roars off down the street.

Gabe, Anna, and I are completely silent, all staring after Rust Bucket's rapidly disappearing taillights. Anna gives another little sob and that galvanizes Gabe into motion. We take her home. Gabe turns on the radio to fill the awkward quiet, but it just makes me more tense.

At Anna's house, she shoves out of the car and gives me a dirty look. "Your whole family's crazy. I should've known better than to date your brother no matter how hot he is."

She stomps inside and I glare after her. "My brother's too good for you!"

Gabe puts a hand on my arm and I rein in my temper. "Sorry. But she's a bitch."

"You want to call it a night?" Gabe asks quietly.

My heart is beating too fast and adrenaline has me wanting to jump from the car and kick down Anna's door. I'm not exactly feeling rational right now.

I blow out a breath and nod. "Yeah. I guess the pictures can wait. We'll go over them tomorrow?"

Gabe squeezes my arm. "Sure thing."

I wish I knew where Emmet's headed and what's going on. The last year, we've barely spoken to each other. I don't know who my brother is anymore and I can't seem to find the words to ask him. But I want to.

CHAPTER TWENTY-SIX

A Miraculous Mess

W hen I step out onto the front porch Thursday morning, I get my first hint that Clemency has morphed into Crazy Town overnight. There's a sign sticking out of the grass by Mrs. Abernathy's mailbox: CAMPING SITE AVAILABLE, $20 A NIGHT. Even more bizarre, there's a neon pink tent sitting like a bloated pimple in the middle of her lawn, and a beat-up, black Volkswagen Beetle is parked at the curb. Mrs. Abernathy hasn't owned a car since she ran over the Shaved Ice Shack last summer and lost her license. I'm still bitter over the lack of snow cones in town.

There's no way my sweet, deaf, older-than-death neighbor is renting out her lawn. And yet there's the sign and there's the tent and there's the car. It's a trifecta of evidence.

I pull out my camera, ready to document this new insanity, but the Polaroid only makes an annoyed whirring noise when I hit the shutter release. I check the number of shots left and sigh. Out of film again. Damn. It'll take a week for new film packs to get here if I order them online. My only other option: persuade Emmet to take me to Bob's Classic Cameras in Ashby on Saturday. Fat chance. Lately, Emmet's harder to find on the weekends than an open liquor store on Sunday.

I'm still working on my mental sales pitch when Emmet strolls out of the house ten minutes later. His hair is sticking up on one side and there are bags under his eyes. Somebody missed his beauty sleep.

"When did you get home last night?" I ask as he eases into the car.

"None of your business," Emmet mumbles.

I don't think there's a single drop of hair gel in his hair this morning. That's almost grounds for a 9-1-1 call. "Tough night?"

"You have no idea."

"Mystery girlfriend dump you?"

Emmet tightens his hands on the steering wheel but finally mutters, "Something like that."

I consider patting his shoulder but the level of awkward in the car is already at Threatcon One proportions. Instead, I say the only thing I can. "Sorry things went to hell."

Emmet's eyebrows go up, and he gives me a suspicious look, doubtless questioning my sincerity. That's what I get for trying to be nice.

Finally he nods and says "Thanks" low enough that I have to lean forward to hear him properly.

I decide not to bring up Bob's Classic Cameras. Maybe he'll be in a better mood tomorrow and I can spring it on him then.

The ride to school is slow and tortuous thanks to traffic. How do city people deal with this crap everyday? We've only been dealing with it for a week and I already want to ram every car on the road. It's almost worth pulling my old bike out of the garage.

I'm still contemplating the joys of road rage when we reach the town center. A giant red banner proclaiming CLEMENCY: THE HOMETOWN OF MIRACLES! is hanging on the park gazebo. Emmet nearly rear-ends the car in front of us, he's so busy staring at the thing.

"What the hell?" I mutter.

Emmet doesn't bother answering. A car horn blares behind us and Emmet casually lifts his middle finger without looking back. The horn blares again.

"We should get out of this mess and take the back roads to school," I say, twisting to glare at the driver behind us. The black Mitsubishi's pinch-faced owner glares back.

Emmet nods.

At the next stop sign, he whips our car to the left and we begin winding through tiny streets and back alleys, headed roughly north. I spot two more tents and more signs. It looks like Mrs. Abernathy is lowballing the others because most are asking $30 a night for camping space. Worse, cars are parked along the side streets and out-of-towners are wandering around, peering into yards like they're strolling through Disneyland. We make only slightly better progress on the back roads and still arrive at school late. Judging by the half-empty parking lot, we aren't the only ones having trouble getting in today.

Gabe isn't waiting for me on the front steps for once, not surprising considering the tardy bell rang ten minutes ago. As I pull one of the main doors open, however, I hear a shout behind me and turn to find Gabe jogging across the parking lot. He looks pissed.

"Five years!" Gabe growls as he stops beside me. "Five years of perfect attendance and some jerk in a Ford nearly runs me over and makes me late."

"You are such a nerd." I soften the comment with a grin.

"I was going for a record!"

"Hey, I'm late too. So are a lot of people. Maybe the school won't count today against you."

More students trickle past, looking grumpy.

Gabe's expression turns thoughtful. "Good point. Maybe Mrs. Winnacker is stuck in traffic."

Unfortunately for Gabe, Mrs. W is waiting for us in homeroom and not interested in excuses. She marks both of us tardy. We sit down just as the morning announcements crackle over the aging PA system.

"Good Morning, Shrenk High Snapping Turtles! There will be a special assembly for all students in the gymnasium at ten this morning."

Gabe and I share a look. Special assemblies mean trouble. This had better not be another one of those teen pregnancy talks they tortured us with last year. Just because a bunch of girls in some other state decided to collectively ruin their lives by getting knocked up, we had to listen to not one, not two, but three intervention sessions telling us about how babies will not solve all our problems.

The assembly is not about teen pregnancy.

Mrs. Candlewhite steps up to the wooden podium that's now sitting beneath the away team basketball hoop. She's dressed in her usual floral dress with white pearls gleaming at her ears and neck. Add a wide brimmed hat and a wooden porch and she'd be the perfect extra in a commercial selling ice tea, the quintessential southern belle. She's a Georgia transport who somehow ended up in our town, and she's never lost the slow twang in her voice.

"Settle down, settle down," Mrs. Candlewhite calls and the murmur of a hundred voices slowly dies away. "Now I'm sure by now you've all seen the news footage, watched a reporter or two, or even been front and center to witness one of the miracles our town has been blessed with. While the miracles have presented a few challenges in recent days, I want to assure you that your classes will remain unaffected by the media interest. There are to be no reporters on campus at any time. I would urge each of you to talk with your parents before giving any interviews. You represent this town in everything you do. Please keep that in mind. We are a strong community, united together, and that is what I want everyone outside Clemency to see whenever they turn on the TV or read a news article. Let's show the world how wonderful our tiny town is and what makes Clemency so special. To that end, Mayor Thompson has provided T-shirts that he would like each of you to wear at the press conference he'll be giving this afternoon. You may pick up a T-shirt in your size on your way out following the assembly."

Mrs. Candlewhite drones on about bus schedules being moved earlier and how it's our responsibility to get to school on time, regardless of road conditions. There's more crap about coming together and presenting a good face to the world. I didn't miss her little jibe about not talking to reporters. Gee, I wonder who that could be aimed at? And while I knew Mayor Thompson was interested in the miracles, this seems like overkill. T-shirts? Really? The scales are definitely tipping in favor of the mayor being behind this whole miracle mess. How long does it take to order several hundred T-shirts?

When we file out of the gym after Mrs. Candlewhite finally stops lecturing us, there's a line of teachers handing out the bright red T-shirts. I ask for a large, and when Mrs. Winnacker hands me a rolled-up shirt, I promptly unfurl it. It has the same slogan as the banner I saw this morning: CLEMENCY: THE HOMETOWN OF MIRACLES!

I shove it in my backpack and shoot an exaggerated eye roll at Gabe. I will *not* be wearing that thing. We have to head in opposite directions for our next classes but I tap the T-shirt he's still holding and say, "Top of the list. We need to find a way into Mayor Thompson's office."

Gabe's mouth falls open, but he doesn't have time to protest. The stream of students exiting the gym carries him away and I head for class. One way or another, I'm getting into that office.

CHAPTER TWENTY-SEVEN

The Proof Is in the Polaroids

The press conference is set for five o'clock so Mayor Thompson can be sure to make the evening news. Unfortunately, my shift at the Gas & Gut also starts at five. That stupid press conference would have been the perfect time to search Mayor Thompson's office. I tried to talk Gabe into doing it solo, but he flat-out refused. I'll keep working on him. I am not giving up such a huge lead. Maybe I can find an invoice that shows Mayor Thompson ordered the T-shirts or the new banners hanging around town before Andy found Baby Cheesus.

Gabe's car is idling in the parking lot when I go off shift at ten.

"How was the press conference?" I ask, sliding into the Taurus.

He shrugs. "Mayor Thompson went on about how small towns are the heart of America. He's creating a tourism board on the town council, and they're going to set up a walking tour of the holy sites around town. Pastor Bobby has agreed to one extra showing of Baby Cheesus a week, on Wednesday evenings. But it'll still be during services. Mayor Thompson invited everyone in the world to come see 'Miraculous Clemency.'"

"What about McJesus and the well?"

"Mr. Henderson isn't letting McJesus go any time soon, but it'll be on the walking tour. Not sure about the well."

"Bet Mayor Thompson regrets not planting those miracles on public property. He'd have had a better chance of getting them and could open a museum."

Gabe presses his lips in a thin line. "We don't know that he planted them."

"He called a press conference. Clearly he's got some bigger agenda. It has to be him. I'm telling you, if we get in his office—"

"I don't want to get arrested for trespassing."

I grumble under my breath but let it drop. I'll sneak in on my own later. Hopefully, there's not an alarm system at the town hall.

"Do you still have the Polaroids?" I ask.

"They're in my backpack. Front pocket."

"Perfect. We can add them to the investigation board."

When we finally get to Gabe's house, his dad is just getting off the phone. Reverend Beaudean grins at the two of us, looking more relaxed and happy than he's been in weeks.

"Evening, Delaney. Bit late for a study session, isn't it?"

I stifle a yawn and give him a sheepish smile. "We won't be long, just need to go over some stuff together."

"Well, don't stay up too late." Reverend Beaudean stops beside Gabe and pats his shoulder. "I got some good news tonight. Melanie agreed to donate the Marion Well to Holy Cross. I already have a spot picked out near the pulpit. Things are looking up for our congregation! Wait until I tell Bobby the news. He can darn well choke on his services-only viewing hours."

I expect Reverend Beaudean to break into a delighted cackle, but he resists. Just barely. He rubs his hands together instead.

"Um, that's great, Dad." Gabe doesn't sound entirely convinced.

Reverend Beaudean gives Gabe a quick hug and then heads down the hallway toward his room, his ratty blue slippers making slapping noises against the linoleum.

"Sounds like Holy Cross will be on the walking tour, as well," Gabe says.

I just nod, still staring after his dad. Guess the church wars are about to heat up again.

Gabe yawns and it sets off a chain reaction, prompting an even bigger yawn from me.

"We don't have to do this tonight," Gabe says. "The Polaroids and our notes will still be around tomorrow."

I wave him away. "We already put it off last night. I just need some coffee."

Gabe frowns, but heads to the kitchen to make a pot anyway.

The coffee helps. A bit. We settle into Gabe's room and he pulls out the photos, passing the stack to me. I flip through them again, looking for the ones directly related to the miracles. There are other pictures mixed in as well: the gazebo in the town center, minus the new banner; Mrs. Abernathy's upside-down flower pot with a daisy growing out of the wrong end. That woman has to be certifiable.

I can't help studying each picture in turn. Trying to see beneath the surface of each small square. My truths. Blurry and messy and real. They're all beautiful in their own way. Even my pictures of the miracles, but it's a different kind of truth I'm looking for now. I pause on an

184

image of Gabe, a silly grin spread across his face and a soda bottle balanced on his head. He's such a goof. I took that picture four days ago in his garage, while we were trying to find the extra controller for his game system.

I'm about to flip to the next picture when something in the background snags my attention. Behind Gabe, a small pile of junk sits on his dad's work bench and a greasy rag hangs off a corner of the table. The soldering iron I saw in Reverend Beaudean's office last weekend is out on the table and the little wood planks are there as well. Three cans of wood stain, recognizable by their obnoxious yellow labels, sit beside the planks.

My breath catches and I look harder at the picture. No freaking way.

"What's up?" Gabe asks, angling closer. "You got naked pictures of the football team in there or something?"

I lift my head and stare at him. There is no way I can tell Gabe about this. Because that isn't a soldering iron in the picture. It's a wood burner. I'm sure of it. And thinking back on the planks of wood in Reverend Beaudean's office—they were the exact same color as Mel's stupid little well. I can't be right. I just can't be. Reverend Beaudean would never do something like this. *Why* would he do something like this?

"Del? Seriously, you're freaking me out. What's the matter?" Gabe steps close and rests a hand on my shoulder.

I don't know what to do. Before I can decide, he plucks the picture out of my hands and studies it. I set the other pictures down on his desk, my hands shaking.

"I can see how my good looks might render you speechless but this isn't even my best shot . . ." Gabe's voice trails off and he squints at the photo.

I think I'm going to throw up.

His eyes dart to me and then back to the picture. He pulls it closer to his face, his nose almost touching the surface. He sees it too. I know he does. And I can tell the exact moment he puts it together. Gabe flings the photo onto his desk and whirls to glare at me. "You think I did this?" he demands in a rough voice.

Crap. Maybe he hasn't put it all together. I never considered for a second that Gabe could be the one faking the miracles. I'd sooner believe I've been faking them in my sleep than accuse him. He's never lied in his life and he'd never do anything to hurt me. I know that with a bone-deep certainty I'm not prepared to let go. Although, five minutes ago I'd have said the same thing about Reverend Beaudean.

"Of course I don't think it's you," I whisper.

Gabe lets out a breath but his frown gets deeper. "Then, what, you think someone's been sneaking into my garage?"

I grasp at the idea like a kid trying to snatch the string of a runaway kite. "Yeah, maybe. Someone could have gotten into the garage, right?"

Gabe narrows his eyes. "Maybe. But that's not what you thought, is it?" He's thinking it through, following the logic trail, and I cringe the moment he connects the dots. His expression goes blank. "You think my dad's been faking the miracles."

"I didn't say that." I force the words out. I want to be a million miles away from here. I want to be standing on the moon, lack of oxygen and everything. I can't breathe right now anyway.

"He'd never do anything like that!" Gabe's voice keeps inching up. Soon he'll blow the roof off the house with the sheer volume. And he's going to wake up his dad. "You see conspiracies where there aren't any. You see fakes where everyone else sees miracles. Don't you dare drag my dad into your witch hunt."

He's pummeling me with words and they hurt. Every single one hurts. Suddenly, I'm furious. I stop cringing and return glare for glare. I'm not some wilting little coward and Gabe is way off base. He's the one flipping out.

"If you're so sure he's not involved then why are you yelling at me? Deep down you know it's a possibility, even if it is a crazy one. I never said your dad faked the miracles. I just want to follow the evidence."

Gabe's shaking and he yanks the papers off the wall, letting them fall to the floor. "I'm done, Del. This is sick."

"You said you'd help," I accuse. "Maybe it was someone sneaking into your garage. At least admit that's possible."

"Fine," Gabe snarls. He sucks in a breath and I can see him fighting to get his temper under control. I've never seen him so mad. It's a little scary. Like maybe I don't know Gabe as well as I thought.

He stalks out of the room. I don't even hesitate before chasing after him. The garage door is already rumbling up, wheels grinding in their tiny metal tracks as I slip inside. Gabe flips on the fluorescent light and it flickers fitfully. To my right a set of plastic shelves hold old paint buckets, garden tools, and a roll of black trash bags that's probably hiding a flourishing spider colony. Half the floor is taken up with boxes and gray plastic storage bins. The area around the work bench is clear, though, an old wooden stool drawn close to the pitted work surface. The wood burner is nowhere in sight and neither are the wooden planks or the cans of wood stain from the Polaroid. There are some fresh gouges in the tabletop, however, and a small burn near one corner, as if something hot was set down.

187

Gabe gestures at the work bench. "Nothing. I told you."

"But it was here." I touch the burn mark.

Gabe frowns. "Maybe. But why would anyone break into my garage? It doesn't make sense."

"I might know where the burner and wood stain are," I mumble.

Gabe turns and gives me a dangerous look. Like he already knows what I'm going to say. "Where?"

"There was a box in your dad's office at the church. I found it when I was looking for the towels on Sunday."

Chapter Twenty-Eight

Lost and Found

Gabe growls under his breath, but turns on his heel and stomps out of the garage and down the driveway. The church is dark when we get there, no cars in the parking lot. Gabe fishes his keys out of his pocket and unlocks the door. We flip on lights as we move through the building, making a straight line for his dad's office.

It's as messy as last time I was in here. Gabe hesitates in the door and I slide past him, focusing on the boxes. Glancing over my shoulder, I wave toward some on my left. "We'll have to check all of them. I can't remember which one had the wood burner and stain."

Gabe moves to a box, pulls back the lid, and pulls out a colorful package of beads with a wooden cross pendant—an activity kit for one of the Sunday school classes. "With evidence this damning, I'm not sure why Dad hasn't turned himself in already."

"Just help me look. I know it was here." I shift one of the boxes closer and begin going through it.

"You're wrong."

"Maybe someone's trying to frame your dad. Ever think of that?" Remembering Reverend Beaudean's face when he found me in this office, I sorta doubt it, though. I keep that thought to myself.

Gabe nods slowly and puts the bead packet back into the box in front of him. "Yeah, I guess so. This is all crazy."

"Things have been crazy since Baby Cheesus showed up. We're rolling with the times," I mutter.

It takes us half an hour to go through all the boxes, but the wood burner and wood stain aren't in any of them. I turn and face Reverend Beaudean's newly cleared desk. We moved each box into a stack after searching it so you can actually see the dark brown desk top now. And the drawers on either side. I'm reaching for the bottom drawer on the right when Gabe grabs my arm.

"What are you doing?" he demands.

"We have to check everything. That means the desk, too."

"You said you saw that stuff in a box. We checked all the boxes. Admit you imagined the whole thing and let's get out of here."

I jerk my arm away and glare at Gabe. "I didn't imagine anything. That stuff could've been moved. It could be in one of the desk drawers."

"There's private stuff in there, church business. You're not going through it!"

"I'm not leaving until we've checked. I know what I saw."

Gabe's face is flushed again and his mouth is a tight, grim line. "Fine. Then get out of the way. I'll check the drawers."

I'm too surprised to object and Gabe nudges me aside, dropping into his father's desk chair. He pulls out the top drawer and rifles through it, finding only paperwork, some highlighters, and a few mismatched paperclips. The next drawer isn't any more exciting. The bottom drawer sticks when Gabe tries to open it and he has to give a good yank to get the thing to move. It's filled with a vertical stack of manila folders.

Gabe's about to slide the drawer closed, but I rest a hand on the drawer edge. "Check behind the folders, there could be something in the back of the drawer."

Gabe huffs out a breath, but he begins pulling the folders out, revealing the dark space behind them. Other than a few dust bunnies as big as cocker spaniels, it's completely empty.

"Satisfied?" Gabe snaps. He piles the folders back into the drawer, one small stack at a time. "I told you this was stupid, there's nothing here." A newspaper cutting flutters down from where it's been clinging to the back of a folder and lands on the desk top.

We both stare at it, falling silent.

It's an obituary: columns of small, neat black type and a tiny picture of Gabe's mom with the title *Montgomery, Lila* just above.

All the breath squeezes out of my lungs, and I shove a hand against my mouth, trying to keep the little air I have left. Even though the last name is wrong, there's no mistaking that picture. In it, Lila is turned away from the camera, looking back over her shoulder with a laugh. Her hair's wild around her face and her eyes are huge and filled with trouble. She looks ready to grab onto life and wring every last drop of fun from it that she can.

Gabe's hand shakes as he traces her name at the top of the page.

I read over his shoulder, skimming the text. "Lila Montgomery, thirty-four, of Plymouth, New Hampshire, died Sunday as the result of a traffic accident on Interstate 93." The worst part, however, is the very last line of the obituary: "Mrs. Montgomery is survived by her husband,

Peter Montgomery. She will be dearly missed." There's no mention of Gabe or his dad. It's as if they never even existed.

How many times over the years have we searched for Lila on the Internet, always coming up blank? Whenever I thought of her, I pictured Lila traveling the country, living her life as wild and carefree as she could. She was the big mystery, the thing that began our friendship.

Something breaks inside me and I struggle to find words that don't exist. My hand squeezes Gabe's shoulder, too hard, but I can't seem to stop. "I'm so sorry," I whisper.

"It's not her," Gabe says in flat voice.

"It has to be," I say gently. "That's your mom's picture and there can't be that many Lilas running around."

"But that's not her last name. My parents never got divorced. There's no way she could have remarried. And what would she be doing in New Hampshire? My mom hated the East Coast."

"I don't know. But your dad had that obituary in his desk. You should ask him about it," I say.

Gabe's head whips around and he glares. "We're here because you think my dad has been lying for weeks, faking miracles and duping people. I'm surprised you think he'd tell the truth about anything."

My face flushes hot, but I don't look away. "I never called your dad a liar."

Gabe makes a disgusted sound. "Not out loud."

He snatches a manila folder off the top of a stack, dumps its contents into the open drawer, and slips the obituary inside. He sweeps the rest of the folders back into the drawer and slams it shut.

I step back as Gabe stalks past me and out of the office. We don't say another word as we leave the church. I want

192

to hug him but I'm afraid of what he'd do. Gabe pauses long enough to lock the doors to the church, but then he's back to stomping away from me again.

"Wait, we need a plan," I call to Gabe's back. My feet are glued to the ground and I rest a hand against the worn bricks by the church entrance.

He stops, but doesn't turn to face me. "I'm going home. You should too."

The words slice into me like scalpels and I stagger back a step, back pressing into the side of the church. He starts walking again and doesn't look back once. Gabe, who's always been there whenever I needed him, walks out on me as though it's the easiest thing in the world.

Chapter Twenty-Nine

Friday, Crappy Friday

I arrive at school Friday minus my backpack. Somehow, with everything going on last night, it got left at Gabe's house. After I left the church, the walk home felt like a thousand miles, and even though I was exhausted when I finally stumbled inside, I tossed and turned for hours.

Gabe isn't waiting for me on the school steps and I doubt it's traffic related this time. I shake it off. He's inside, that's all. He probably had to grab something from his locker. But I don't spot Gabe in the halls either. Maybe he skipped school. There's a first time for everything and finding out your mom is dead is a pretty good reason to ditch.

All around me students chatter and gossip. Whispers of miracles and divine cures fill the halls. Pretty much business as usual. Except for the miracle merchandise. I see a half dozen T-shirts mentioning Baby Cheesus and only a handful are the ones Mayor Thompson passed out. I SAW CHEESUS buttons are attached to backpacks and baseball caps. Anna is even showing off a Cheesus key chain.

Our town is officially a freak show.

Seconds before the tardy bell rings, Gabe dashes through the door of homeroom and takes his seat. He drops my backpack at my feet without looking at me.

Despite the risk of Mrs. Winnacker's wrath, I scrawl a quick note and try to pass it to Gabe under his desk. He ignores me, acting like he has no idea what I'm doing. When the bell rings, he's out the door before I can say a word.

I stare after him, feeling like cement is filling my lungs. We've never done the no-talking thing. Never had a fight that lasted more than a few hours. I don't know what to do. What if he's decided our friendship isn't worth the trouble?

By lunch break, I'm ready to start screaming in the middle of the hall if it'll get Gabe to look at me. Wendy bounces over as I enter the lunch room and I snarl, "Leave me alone."

"Well," she huffs. "That was rude. I'll pray for you to develop a better attitude."

"So not gonna happen," I mutter, scanning the room for Gabe. I spot him and stalk over, slamming my books down on the table. "I am done with the silent treatment. You want to end us? Fine. Have the courage to say it to my face."

The kids at the tables on either side of us go quiet and I can feel them all staring at me. My world is crumbling to bits and they can jump off a damn cliff for all I care. In this moment, Gabe's the only thing that matters.

He stares up at me. There are dark patches under both his eyes and a bit of stubble scattered on his chin. He looks as if he's missed a couple nights' sleep instead of only one. The anger and tension ease a little inside of me. I want to hug him and say it'll be all right, even if it's a lie.

"What are you talking about?" Gabe asks in a quiet voice, glancing at the people staring at us.

I grit my teeth and sit down, back statue straight. "Don't pretend you haven't been avoiding me all morning. I get that you're pissed at me, and yeah, you've got reasons. But I never figured you for a coward. If our friendship is over, then fine. I'll deal. But you look me in the eye and say it." My words are hissed out, hard, tossed like rocks between us. They burn my tongue until my mouth is numb.

Gabe's lips tighten and he gives me a flat look. "You'll deal? So you're fine with not being friends anymore? Six years and you can walk away that easy?"

"I'm not the one walking away! I never turned my back on you, not once, and I never would."

"That's rich." Gabe leans forward, voice dropping even lower, every word precise. "When Claire died you ran away from me so fast I never had a chance to catch you. You decided you didn't need anyone or anything and certainly not me. I spent months trying to get you to talk. You couldn't be bothered. It was easier to get drunk, smoke pot, and pretend nothing was wrong. So who's the coward? And when you came back from that little insanity trip, I was still here, waiting for you. You act like you're the only one who ever lost someone. My mom left me behind like a pile of trash. She erased me from her life and I didn't even get a mention in her obituary."

I open my mouth but Gabe makes a sharp cutting motion with his hand. "No. This time *you* listen." His voice drops even lower. "I found out my mom is dead. And according to you there's a good chance my dad's a fraud. I gave you months to figure yourself out and you can't even give me a handful of fucking hours?"

It's the f-bomb more than anything that chokes the words in my throat. Gabe hardly ever curses. Especially not an f-bomb. He's too much a preacher's kid for that. With a sick feeling, I realize he's right. About all of it. I've been so wrapped up in my hurt and my pain, I haven't had time for anything else. Not him. Not my family. His world is crashing around his head and instead of trying to be understanding, I'm pissed he needs a while to figure it out. Hurt he's not talking to me. I feel as big as a mosquito and just as welcome.

"I'm sorry," I whisper. I drop my eyes and take a deep breath, shoving the hurt down, the guilt. If Gabe needs time, I'll give it to him.

I move to get up and Gabe grabs my arm, stopping me. "You want a ride home tonight, after your shift?" His voice is gruff.

I meet his gaze uncertainly. "Sure."

He squeezes my arm gently and drops it. "We'll talk then."

I nod. I'll wait all night for him if I have to.

A wave of whispers follows me as I walk out of the cafeteria, every student in the place talking about the very public and unprecedented fight Gabe and I just had. A dozen rumors are being born right now and I'll bet everyone thinks we were fighting over the miracles. For the first time in weeks, the miracles are the last thing on my mind.

That night, Gabe's five minutes late picking me up from the Gas & Gut. I'm in the middle of a full-blown panic attack—sweaty palms, shortness of breath, and extreme tunnel vision—by the time his car pulls up. I wrench the door open and fling myself inside before he's even had a chance to put the car in park.

"Something on fire?" Gabe asks quietly, turning off the motor.

I shake my head and settle my backpack at my feet, finally feeling like I can breathe again. He showed up.

The silence grows into something living. The car hasn't moved and Gabe's hands are well away from the ignition, resting in his lap. I break under the weight of all the words neither of us are brave enough to say. My eyes are blurry with tears when I lean over, armrest digging into my side, and hug him. He doesn't hug me back, just sits bonelessly.

"I'm sorry," I whisper. I feel like I've said those words so many times today but they won't stop, pouring out and wrapping around us like a noose. I'm not sure what I'm apologizing for: accusing his dad, his mom being dead, or having been such an awful friend this past year. Maybe all of it.

Seconds, minutes, maybe hours later, Gabe winds his arms around me and we cling together. Gabe pulls away first and I let him.

"He knew." Gabe's voice sounds like rocks are stuck in his throat. "All this time, my dad knew and he never said a word."

I expect tears, but Gabe's face is hard.

"What are you going to do?" I ask softly.

"I'm going to make him tell me the truth." Gabe clenches his fists and glares at the dashboard.

For a moment, I consider grabbing the keys and throwing them out the window, trying to keep Gabe here before he does something he regrets. But I can't blame him for wanting to confront his dad. Isn't searching for the truth what I've been doing for months? Floundering through the dark to try to find something real to hold on to. First with Claire, and then with the miracles. And what about

Gabe? What truth does he need to find? I think about the Polaroid with those wood panels in Gabe's garage, the wood stain I saw in Mr. Beaudean's office. I thought the truth would help the world make sense again, but instead, everything's been twisted inside out.

I put a hand on Gabe's arm. "I want to come with you."

"Why? So you can accuse my dad of faking the miracles?" Gabe pulls his arm away and it feels like a slap.

"No! This isn't about the stupid miracles. It's just . . ." I flounder, trying to find the right words but they aren't there. I settle for telling him the things I should have said a long time ago. "I wish you'd been with me when Mom called to tell me Claire was dead. And I know that's not your fault, it's mine. I shut you out. I can't roll back the clock, but I can be there for you now. With this."

Gabe shakes his head. "This isn't the sort of conversation you invite friends to."

"I know. But it is the kind of conversation maybe you need to talk about afterward. You don't have to do this alone. Please. I'll stay out of the way," I wheedle, keeping any trace of pity or worry out of my voice. "I can hang out on the porch or hide in your room. I—"

Gabe holds up a hand. "Fine. But we're doing this tonight. I waited six years, I'm not waiting another day."

Chapter Thirty

Late Night Confrontations

O nce again, time is bending and warping around me, only now it's cramming our ten-minute drive into a handful of seconds. We pull up in front of Gabe's house long before either one of us is ready.

Gabe lets the car idle, sliding it into park. Another long, awkward silence fills the interior, but this time I don't bother breaking it. He takes slow, deep breaths, eyes fixed on the house. Finally he turns the car off and reaches into the backseat for the manila folder from last night. When he gets out of the car, the door slams shut behind him, loud as a gunshot.

I wince, but get out as well. Nausea rolls in my stomach and I shiver as I follow Gabe. I'm responsible for this mess. If I hadn't insisted we go to his dad's office, he never would have found his mom's obituary.

When we reach his front porch, Gabe pauses, a hand resting against the door. "You sure you want to hang around? This isn't going to be pretty."

"Yeah. I've got your back."

Gabe nods his head once. "Fine. But no butting in. You stay in my room."

"Sure." I almost mean it. But if Gabe needs me, awkward as it's going to be, I'll come tearing out of his room faster than a twister through a trailer park.

Inside, the low rumble of a TV announcer fills the living room and I can see the flickering light from the screen reflected against the white walls. It dances on the edge of a framed picture in the hall, red-haired Lila holding a tiny baby and grinning at the camera. Her head is cocked to the side at a playful angle and she looks on the verge of laughter. Gabe stares at the picture and then yanks it off the wall, putting it face down on the entry table.

Reverend Beaudean's voice booms out, "Gabe?"

I bolt for Gabe's room. When I'm safe behind his door, I press my head and back against the thin wood. Gabe doesn't bother keeping his voice low.

"I know about Mom."

"What are you talking about? Did your mother send a postcard finally?" Reverend Beaudean's voice sounds confused, groggy with sleep. He must've been napping in front of the TV when we arrived.

"Stop lying!" Gabe yells. "She's dead and you've known about it for years."

"What on earth are you talking about?" Mr. Beaudean's voice is higher, all sleepiness gone.

"This!" There's a pause and I imagine Gabe brandishing the obituary at his dad.

"Where did you get that?" Mr. Beaudean demands.

"From your office. Where you've been hiding it. How long have you known, Dad? How long have you been lying to me?"

I pick at a loose thread on the arm of my T-shirt, hands shaking. Part of me wants to be out there beside Gabe, demanding answers. Reverend Beaudean's always seemed like the perfect parent, if a bit absentminded. He never would have run off the way my dad did. He'd have stuck by his family. But maybe I was wrong. If Reverend

201

Beaudean could lie about Lila's death, if he could fake those miracles and not say a word, maybe he was never the person I thought.

"Gabe, you don't understand," Mr. Beaudean says.

"Then tell me! I deserve to know that at least." Gabe's voice is hoarse now, like he's holding back tears.

"I'm so sorry, son. I couldn't bear to break your heart any more than your mama already had. You took her leaving hard, so tore up inside you had nightmares for months. You watched me like a hawk every time I stepped out of a room."

Gabe interrupts. "You pretended she might come back. You helped me write letters, pick out Christmas cards. You made that stupid box for me to put them all in, knowing she was dead."

"I didn't know she was dead until weeks after it happened, when a lawyer contacted me, and that was a full year after she left us. You were just beginning to sleep through the night again. Most days, hope's the only thing that got you up in the mornings." The reverend's husky voice is pleading and so low I can barely hear him.

I press the back of my head harder against the door and close my eyes. I don't want to listen in, but at the same time, I don't want to miss a word.

"Hope's the only thing that kept you sane," Mr. Beaudean continues. "It's the most powerful thing in the world and after what Lila did, I couldn't take that away from you. You'd already lost so much. I told myself I'd tell you when you were a little older. When you could handle the news. But it never seemed like the right time. And eventually, I'd waited too long. How could I tell you she'd been gone all these years? I didn't ever want you to look at me the way you're looking at me now. You're all I've got, Gabe. I didn't want to lose you as well."

Gabe makes an angry noise, half under his breath but audible even through the door. "I had a right to know. When it happened. But you kept right on lying. How am I ever supposed to trust you again?"

"I wanted to protect you."

"You were a coward. Too afraid to admit you couldn't control her because maybe then I'd start getting ideas too."

"I've never tried to control you or forced you to do anything!"

"No. Nothing straightforward like that. You've manipulated me and everyone else instead. Just like you did with Mom. Maybe she left because she couldn't stand the games you play with people."

"What are you talking about?" Mr. Beaudean sounds genuinely mystified. I'm kinda wondering where Gabe is headed with this as well.

"The miracles, Dad! I know you faked the whole thing."

Chapter Thirty-One

A Plea for Clemency

Holy shit. I never thought Gabe would actually confront his dad about the miracles.

"Gabriel Beauregard Beaudean, you better explain yourself this instant and exactly what you're accusing me of." Mr. Beaudean's voice is flat and stiff as a fence post.

"Del found proof. She has a picture of the wood planks from the wishing well after you'd begun painting them." Gabe sounds calm. Too calm.

I wince, uncomfortable at being dragged into the conversation. Which makes me consider, for the first time, what we'd have done if I'd found more proof that it really is Reverend Beaudean faking the miracles. Could I have confronted Gabe's dad? Face to face? Could I have accused a man who's served me hot cocoa, driven us to the movies, listened to made-up stories of daring adventures, and patiently allowed us to wreck his kitchen while making chocolate chip cookies? My stomach gives a tiny lurch.

Mr. Beaudean takes so long to answer I start to wonder if he walked out of the room and left Gabe standing there.

"I might have guessed it'd be Del who figured things out. That girl can't ever leave well enough alone."

I barely recognize Mr. Beaudean's voice. He was pleading and upset with an edge of anger when talking about

Lila. Now he sounds like he ran a double marathon and can't catch his breath, exhaustion coating every word. I wrap my arms around my chest and squeeze. I want to run away as fast as I can, turn into Superman and fly backward around the Earth so I can turn back time. This is worse than not knowing.

How could it be Mr. Beaudean? That question and a dozen others get me moving. I stop hugging myself and pull Gabe's door open, leaving the false safety of his room. My feet are on autopilot as I zombie shuffle into the living room.

Gabe and Mr. Beaudean are standing a few feet apart, Gabe with his mouth hanging open as he stares at his dad, Mr. Beaudean rubbing a hand over his face.

"Why?" I croak out. There are tears clogging my throat.

Both Gabe and his dad swivel to face me.

"Del." Mr. Beaudean sighs and his shoulders slump. "Lurking in doorways is a nasty habit."

"So's lying." I fling the words at him, half hurt, half furious.

Gabe moves to stand next to me and my heart turns into a hot air balloon, swooping up into my throat. He might still be mad, but he's here beside me the way we've always been. He's got my back and I've got his.

"Let's sit down," Mr. Beaudean says. "I can't abide all this looming about." He waves toward the couch and eases himself into his chair. His fingers pluck at the threadbare seat arm.

The chair is a ratty brown thing, lumpy from years of use, yellowed stuffing visible through a small hole on the cushion front. Sometimes, when Gabe and I have movie marathons, his dad joins us, always in that chair. This feels like a pantomime of those nights; a sick, twisted parody where we're each taking our place but nothing is what it should be.

I drop onto the couch. My knees are a bit wobbly anyway. Gabe hesitates but sits beside me, twisting to face his dad.

"You're admitting it? You faked the miracles?" I whisper.

Mr. Beaudean shakes his head. "Not all of them."

"Because that makes it better!" Gabe leans forward, glaring at his dad. "What else have you been lying about? Any other dead relatives you want to mention?"

"That's enough, Gabe!" Mr. Beaudean's weariness slides away and he's got his stern preacher face on again. "You have every right to be upset, but pettiness won't help the situation. I had reasons for what I did, whether you agree with them or not."

"What possible reason could you have for lying to the entire town?" Gabe says.

"Wake up, son. We can barely keep the church open. The board voted to stop half our ministries because there aren't enough funds. Holy Cross has been in financial trouble for a while, but not like this. Ballard isn't exactly a rich county and there are so many people who need our help. People who don't have anyone else to turn to. Mrs. Deardly with her fifteen cats, more concerned with feeding them than herself. Ida Wentzel, who just had her sixth child and can't even afford diapers because Kenny drinks away his paycheck.

"There are people needing help on every farm and in every house. And we can't do anything about it. I can't afford to run the meal truck because the cost of gas is too high. The church roof is caving in, but all we've been able to do is patch it for two years now. This community has never had much to give, but they've done their best and we put their tithes to good use doing God's work.

"Then, all of a sudden, half our congregation disappears over to St. Andrew's after some ridiculous cheese wheel. St. Andrew's tithes doubled. Bobby was bragging about it. But does he funnel that money back into the community? No, he buys a fancy glass case for that cheese wheel, prints color programs, and orders a new microphone for Sunday services. I'm not saying Bobby's a bad person, but he focuses more on his church than his congregation.

"I thought the cheese wheel situation would blow over but it's been weeks of half-filled services and no end in sight. Weeks without being able to scrape enough together for the work we normally do."

Gabe opens his mouth to interrupt but Reverend Beaudean holds up a hand and stares Gabe down.

"You want to know why, then let me finish. I thought long and hard about what needed to be done. Prayed for hours. But I couldn't see any other way through. Not without giving up completely. No one would listen to reason, not when talk shows were calling Bobby, not when every stubbed toe was cause for a visit to that blighted cheese wheel. I thought, if I found our own miracle, something we could use to take the attention off Bobby's cheese wheel, everything would even out. So I painted Jesus's face on the drive-through window. I thought for sure Robert Henderson would let me have the thing when he found it, but he outright refused, despite six years of friendship."

Mr. Beaudean continues, leaning forward, face flushed and earnest. "But I was right about another miracle taking the focus off the cheese wheel. If I'd been able to get Robert to let me have that window everything would've been fine. I never thought he'd be so greedy, wanting to use the window to draw people into a restaurant of all things." Mr. Beaudean's outrage is kinda funny. Guess he doesn't see the irony in what he's saying. He wanted to use McJesus to lure people in as well—he just wasn't trying to get them to buy jumbo fries with it. "So I had to figure out another miracle, one I could be sure would come to Holy Cross."

"So you faked the wishing well," I blurt out. Mr. Beaudean jumps a little, as if he's forgotten I'm there. His frown adds more wrinkles to his forehead.

"Yes." His voice is subdued now. "I made the wishing well panel and attached it. Melanie has been coming to Holy Cross since she was little and she has a good heart. I knew she wouldn't keep the well for personal gain."

"And her mom flipping out on live TV?" I accuse. "That was collateral damage?"

Mr. Beaudean slumps lower in his chair. "I didn't realize how bad things had become. Melanie never said, and LuAnne seemed rational the last time I stopped by for a visit."

"What happened to trusting God?" Gabe shifts next to me, mouth puckering into a sour expression. "How many sermons have you given telling people to be patient, that God acts in his own time. Did you mean any of it? Did you even listen to the words you were saying?"

"Sometimes God needs help. Aren't missionaries passing out food to the poor doing God's work? Doctors providing free vaccines in Africa? Congregations coming together to build homes and schools for the needy in South America? Aren't all of these people acting in God's name to help make the world a better place? Our parish, your neighbors, Gabe, they need us and I can't help them. How could I stand by and watch all our good work disappear because for a brief time our congregation was seduced away?"

"None of those missionaries or doctors used fake miracles to do God's work," Gabe snaps.

Mr. Beaudean looks stricken, but he squares his shoulders. "I don't expect you to understand. You're too young and you haven't seen enough of the world. Sometimes sacrifices have to be made."

"Like the truth?" I half whisper, still reeling.

It feels like there's a caged lion sitting next to me, Gabe is so tense. He clenches and unclenches his hands. "What happens now? Because it's not a secret anymore. Del and I know."

I wince, but Gabe has a point. What *do* we do now? I never planned further than finding out who was faking the miracles.

Mr. Beaudean turns so he's looking directly at me. "You understand what I'm saying, don't you, Del? You can see how important it is to help this community?"

I shake my head, heart breaking. "Everything's a lie. How could that ever be good?" Turns out I was right and miracles aren't real. I expect to feel triumph, smugness, something. Instead, I feel hollow.

"Del?" Gabe asks sharply. He takes my arm. It's only then I realize I'm crying.

I can count on one hand the number of times I've cried since Claire died.

"Are you okay?" Gabe asks and I give a watery laugh. His life just fell apart and he wants to know if I'm okay. That thought helps me pull it together.

"I'm fine. I mean, I knew the miracles were being faked. I just wasn't ready for it to be . . ." My voice trails off and I look at Reverend Beaudean.

He seems so sad, but his jaw is set, and he's watching Gabe and me closely. I'm not sure what he sees that makes the lines in his face deepen.

"I think the three of us need to discuss everything that's happened and what we're going to do," Mr. Beaudean says.

Gabe snorts. "What's to discuss? You need to publicly apologize for faking the miracles and lying to everyone."

Mr. Beaudean shakes his head. "If I admit I faked the miracles, we'll lose Holy Cross and be forced to leave town. And what about this community? They believe, with all their hearts, that God has blessed them. They've been given hope. You snatch that away and it's going to breed a whole lot of despair. Our church does so much good. This will wipe all of that away."

My vocal cords have seized up, strangling me, and Mr. Beaudean's words repeat over and over in my head. They wouldn't really have to leave, would they? I can't lose Gabe. I can't.

"What do you expect Del and me to do? Lie to everyone? Pretend the miracles are real? Pretend you're not a fraud?"

"I expect you to put the needs of your community first." Mr. Beaudean's hands tighten on the arms of his chair, his voice hoarse. "Think before you do anything, and pray. God will guide you to the right decision. Sometimes the world isn't black and white, it's every shade of gray, and you have to decide which is the least evil to achieve the most good."

"Don't you dare bring God into this. If you believed, truly believed, like you've always told me to, you wouldn't have faked anything. You wouldn't have needed to."

Their words whip back and forth and Gabe's are barbed, designed to draw blood. I know it's more than the fake miracles, it's everything to do with his mom and the lies upon lies. I can hear the thread of accusation underlying each syllable. He says his dad should have trusted God, but what he means is that his dad should have trusted him.

Part of me agrees with Reverend Beaudean. Not with what he did. But I can understand why he felt he needed to fake the miracles. When God is silent, how can we not act on our own?

I tune back into the argument when I hear my name again.

"And Del?" Gabe asks. He squeezes my hand and I realize that at some point he twined our fingers together. "Does she get a say in whether we're going to lie for you?"

"I'm not asking you to lie." Mr. Beaudean leans forward, hands gripped together and resting on his knees. "All I'm asking is that you not announce to the world that the miracles are fake. Clemency needs them to be real and our congregation needs them too. Think about the damage you'll do!"

"No more miracles." My words are so low it's a wonder anyone can hear them. Gabe swivels to stare at me and Mr. Beaudean goes still. "Not one more," I add.

"Of course not," Mr. Beaudean says. He clears his throat, straightening a little. "We have the well now, that's all Holy Cross needed."

"Are you serious?" Gabe demands, still looking at me. "You're going to let it go?" He loosens his grip and our hands slip apart. My fingers rest in my lap and I wish I had something to hold on to: my camera, Gabe's hand, or a safety net.

I shake my head. "It's not okay. It's never going to be okay. But your dad losing his job and the two of you moving away is worse."

"You spent weeks trying to figure this stuff out." He's looking at me the same way he was looking at his dad a minute ago. Betrayed.

"What am I supposed to do, Gabe?" My voice is bordering on hysterical. "Who am I going to tell? Call up the *Weekly World News* and offer them an exclusive? 'Extra, Extra, God Doesn't Exist, Miracles Proven Fake.'"

"Of course God exists." Mr. Beaudean slips back into his preacher's voice, gently chiding. "And there *are* real miracles. Sometimes the Lord just needs a little help."

"Don't," I snap, all hysteria gone. "You don't get to say those words to me. Not after this. I won't tell anyone about the fake miracles, but I won't help cover up any more lies. And I won't listen to any lectures about God." I get up before Gabe or his dad can say anything else. "I'm gonna head home. I'll see you tomorrow," I tell Gabe and hurry out.

As I pull the front door closed behind me, I can hear Reverend Beaudean's voice, more tired than ever, "Lord, how did I make such a mess of things?"

Chapter Thirty-Two

The Lies We Tell Ourselves

The house is dark when I get home, but Rust Bucket is sitting out front. I'm about to walk past when a sudden movement makes me stop. There's someone sitting inside. Actually, two someones. And they're kissing. I'm ready to shrug it off, except there's something odd about that second figure. I take a step closer, totally spying on my brother and not even caring. I need the distraction just now.

The two figures break apart and Emmet sees me through the passenger side window. His face goes blank and then panic sweeps over his features. Beside him, the guy he's been making out with twists around to face me. The *guy* he's just been making out with. My brother was frenching some random dude in our driveway. I back away and then bolt for the front door.

"Del!" Emmet calls, but he doesn't follow me and I don't stop. I slam my way inside and stand in the entryway, chest heaving. A moment later, Rust Bucket roars to life and tears away from the house.

I climb the stairs feeling like my shoes are coated in concrete. What is happening to my life? Mr. Beaudean is a lying, miracle-faking jerk and apparently my girl-crazed brother has decided to start dating boys. Or at least locking lips with them.

There isn't any peace in my room and my mind won't stop whirring around, trying to figure out how I'm going to claw my way back to normal after everything that's happened. I catch sight of my blue notebook. It's filled with notes about the miracles, motives, suspects. I snatch it up and begin ripping out pages. I keep tearing until my bed and the floor are covered in ragged white confetti, until even the best puzzle master couldn't put the pieces back together. Then I start on the Polaroids. I yank out pins and let the pictures fall to the floor, stepping on them as I reach for more. I don't stop until my walls are bare and empty, my floor completely covered with battered, crumpled photos. There aren't any truths left in the world. Even pictures lie.

When there's nothing left to tear down or rip up, I flop onto my bed, trying to catch my breath. The quiet feels like it's going to swallow me whole. I stay that way for a long time, but I can't sleep. Finally, I give up and head for the living room. Maybe some mindless late-night TV will make my head stop spinning.

I'm passing Mom's room when I notice the light spilling out from under her door. She must have left the light on when she headed out earlier. How times have changed. She used to chase Claire and me through the house turning off lights and lecturing us about all the electricity we were wasting.

I consider leaving a snarky note on her bedside table but decide to just turn off the light. Her door creaks when I open it. Mom looks up from where she's sitting on the bed and I freeze in the doorway.

"Del?" Her voice is husky and uncertain.

Mom's hair frizzes wildly around her face like a mad scientist and she's wearing her robe. Her eyes are red-rimmed, nose bright as a cherry. Used tissues lie on the bed beside her and one of the old photo albums is balanced in her lap, the faux leather cover just visible in all its gaudy glory.

When I was little, I used to help Mom put the pictures in, sliding each image into its plastic sleeve. She'd laugh and say things like "Look at your father's hair, it's sticking straight up." Or "Do you remember when Pops gave you that sour licorice and you threw up after eating the entire bag?" Yes, my mother actually has a picture of my green face, lips stained with sour sugar just before I blew chunks all over the kitchen. Our photo albums are filled with gems like that, enough blackmail potential for a lifetime.

I haven't looked at them in years.

"Aren't you working tonight?" I blurt.

Mom shakes her head and runs a hand over the page she was looking at. "No, I called in sick."

Mom never calls in sick. Never. The Everything Store has this insane sick policy that basically means if you call in sick more than twice you get fired. Last spring, Mom went to work even though she had a super high fever and sounded like she was about to hack out a lung. If she's home now, whatever she has must be serious.

"What's wrong?" I demand. "Did you see a doctor?" The C word hangs in the back of my mind, as it so often does, and I covertly eye Mom, trying to spot any obvious bruises or lumps.

"I just needed a night at home." Mom sighs and glances down at the photo album again. "I can't believe it's been a year."

My stomach uncoils, but only slightly. Of course Mom would be obsessing over Claire again. Is there anything else in the world? I'm still a shadow person where Mom's concerned and the only one who matters, who ever mattered, is darling Claire. At least my mother's still predictable.

"I ditched school for an entire week last spring," I say. Mom looks back up, forehead creasing. "What?"

"And last month, I drank all the vodka from Dad's liquor cabinet and spent the night puking in your rosebushes. But you wouldn't know that either. I know it's been a year because *I've* been here this whole time."

"You drank your father's vodka?" Her mouth is drawn down, puckered with confusion. She's looking at me like I just told her I'm an alien with three heads.

"Yes. And all the brandy. It was nasty but I choked it down. And Emmet's been sneaking out. Ever wonder where he's at, because I'm pretty sure it's not a pep rally. In fact, I can guarantee you'd be shocked at the things he's getting up to. You used to care what happened to us. Now all you do is sit around and cry over Claire's baby pictures and how you lost your perfect little angel. I lost my whole family."

Mom's eyes fill with tears again and she snuffles, snatching a tissue to dab at her nose. "Oh, Del, honey. I'm so sorry."

I back up a step, shaking my head. "You know the worst part?" My voice is verging on a scream but to hell with it. It's been a long couple of days and I've earned a meltdown or two. "I actually thought things were going to get better. You said we'd start having family dinners again. You acted like maybe you were done with the zombie impersonation you've been doing. Then along come those stupid miracles and you're back to Claire pity party central. They're not even real. I have proof the miracles are fake. But I bet you don't care about that either. Because all that matters is maybe some hunk of processed cheese might have saved Claire. News flash, Mom: nothing would've saved Claire, just like nothing's going to save this family."

I whirl and walk away. I can't believe I ever thought proving the miracles are fake would fix things. Sometimes broken things just stay broken.

I lock my door behind me and fling myself on the bed, burying my face in a pillow. I am not crying. And even if I am, there's no one here to see.

My doorknob rattles and Mom's voice drifts through the door. "Del? Please open up."

I shove my face harder into the pillow and try to block out her voice.

It's quiet for a long minute. She's probably back crying over the photo albums again.

"I'm sorry," Mom whispers. So faint. But I can hear her.

I turn my face to the side and stare at the closed door.

"I screwed up," Mom continues. "I didn't mean to push you and Emmet away. I never wanted to lose you too. Things will get better. I promise, Delli. And no more raiding Dad's liquor cabinet. I'm emptying any bottles that are left down the drain right now. I will try, honey. I will try to be better. To be here."

She pauses and I can hear her breathing on the other side of the door. But I don't trust her anymore. Not after this year. Not after the past few weeks. She probably has some deep, dark secret she's hiding too.

"I love you," Mom whispers, and then there's the shuffle of feet as she walks back to her room.

I turn my head away and draw in a deep breath, ignoring the tears burning their way down my face. I am not crying for Mom or myself or Gabe or how screwed up life is. I'm not crying at all. If I keep telling myself that, it might eventually be true.

Chapter Thirty-Three

Little Girl Lost

Saturday morning, I wake up to the smell of pancakes. At first I'm sure it's a hallucination. We haven't had pancakes in years. Photos slide under my feet when I walk to my closet. I don't bother cleaning up the mess. It feels fitting, somehow. The first honest thing in a while. After I'm dressed, I follow my nose downstairs.

Mom's sitting at the table, dressed in a yellow sundress and slathering butter on a stack of pancakes at least a foot tall. Clearly she's been replaced by a clone. She glances up, butter knife poised over the pancakes, and gives me a nervous smile.

"Morning, sleepyhead," Mom says. "I thought it'd be nice if we had breakfast together. Why don't you go wake up Emmet and we'll all sit down together. I think the three of us need to talk."

Just then a door bangs open upstairs. There's a groan and the sound of someone throwing up violently. I'm pretty sure Emmet didn't make it to the bathroom.

"Don't think that's gonna work out for you," I mutter.

The pancakes smell so good. But I cannot be bought with pancakes, no matter how delicious they look. I'm sure by tonight she'll be back in her bedroom sobbing again, this little overture forgotten. How can I trust her?

"I hate pancakes," I lie. "And I'm late for my shift at the Gas & Gut."

Mom scowls and her eyebrows lower to battle position. I bolt for the front door before she can stop me. I'm glad I don't have to face Emmet yet. I don't know what to say.

I wasn't just lying about the pancakes. I never work Saturdays; that's Andy's shift. But what else am I going to do today? I'd feel weird showing up on Gabe's doorstep after everything that's happened and calling him doesn't feel quite right either. I can't stay at home and I've got nowhere else to be.

I call Andy and beg to take over his shift. He pretends like he's reluctant but finally mumbles something about a pasture party that evening and agrees. I ignore his mention of picking up party favors. He's not talking about balloons or a piñata.

The store is busy all day, packed with people looking for cheese wheels, Cheesus buttons, and the tacky rubber Cheesus bracelets Ken just ordered last week. It's a steady distraction from my thoughts.

A little after five, Maybelle Jensen totters in, sucking her false teeth and narrowing her eyes at me as she clears the front door. "I thought Ken switched his hours on Sunday so you could attend church. Why haven't I seen you at St. Andrew's?"

I smile sweetly. "Now you know I've been attending Holy Cross, Mrs. Jensen."

"There are big things happening at St. Andrew's, girl." Maybelle raps her swollen knuckles on the counter. "Big things. The Lord's at work, healing the sick and bringing comfort to his people. Why, if that cheese wheel had been found a few years ago, I bet that sister of yours would have turned out fine."

I grit my teeth. I know Maybelle's the one that's been filling Mom's head with nonsense about the miracles and Claire. I'm so busy fuming I only half hear what she's saying, but the word cancer drags my attention back to her.

"What?" I interrupt. "What did you say?"

"I said there was a girl sick with the cancer like your sister. Her family drove all the way from Amarillo so she could be healed. Pale little thing, skinny and near bald. Makes a person's heart shudder just looking at her. Bobby held a special prayer session at the sanctuary last night, laid her hands on the cheese wheel and I do believe I saw a golden glow around the both of them. Mark my words, she'll be right as rain in no time."

My breath catches in my throat as I stare at Maybelle. I knew people were visiting the cheese wheel and then claiming to be healed. But that's minor stuff. A sprained ankle, a cold, a nasty skin rash. But no one terminally ill.

"Are they staying in town?" I ask, knotting my hands around a cleaning rag.

Maybelle breaks off mid-word and stares at me. "What, dear?"

"The family with the sick little girl, where are they staying?"

"How would I know that?" She sniffs. "They might be at the Ford dealership, Hershel's renting out spaces for RVs."

Maybelle rattles on for a while but I've stopped listening. I give a halfhearted smile when she finally gives up and leaves. All the way out of the store, Maybelle mutters about the horrible manners of young people today.

When Ken shows up to take the evening shift at six, I explain about swapping with Andy. Ken just waves me away and says not to mess with his schedule again without warning him. I nod, trying to look contrite, and scurry out the door. The spot where Gabe usually parks is empty. I never called to tell him I'd be here. Of course he hasn't called or texted me all day either.

I consider going home but I turn toward the Ford dealership instead.

I spot the family long before I reach the dealership and the rows of RVs now filling the lot where shiny new trucks used to crouch. The three of them move slowly, inching along on the opposite side of the road. The dad is hunched, his clothes wrinkled and face drawn as he pushes a small wheelchair. He looks as if he's been walking across the Sahara and hasn't had a drop of water the entire way. Beside him, his wife chatters in a high-pitched voice, kinky blonde curls bobbing as she smiles and gestures with her hands. Her movements are jerky and false. There's an oxygen tank strapped to the back of the wheelchair, as big as the girl riding in front of it.

The girl is so small. Younger than Claire was when she was diagnosed. Nine maybe? In the cancer ward, when I visited Claire, half the kids were bald, a few with odd patches of hair clinging to their heads and a few looking so normal you'd never know they were sick. This girl has hair that brushes the tips of her ears, shorter than a pixie cut and pale as dandelion fluff. It surprises me.

A bald head is the first thing you think of when someone says cancer. Like you can't have the one without the other. When Claire lost all her hair, including her eyebrows and eyelashes, I used to draw silly shapes on her with different colored eyebrow pencils and then she'd draw squiggly pictures on my cheeks. I'd pull out my camera and we'd lean in close together, her chemical breath brushing my cheek as I snapped pictures.

Is it better or worse that the girl looks nothing like Claire? It still hurts to see her.

The front wheel of the wheelchair catches on a crack in the sidewalk and the entire thing lurches sideways. The dad quickly yanks the chair upright, and the little girl clings to the armrests. I'm across the street before I can reconsider.

"Are you all right? Do you need help?" I'm out of breath, and not from my short sprint.

The woman is bent over, fussing at her daughter and smoothing a hand down the girl's bony arm. She looks up at me, fake smile tacked in place. "We're fine, dear. Thanks so much for offering."

The man nods.

I take a step back, regretting my impulse to run over here. It's worse beside them. I can smell the same antiseptic chemical scent wafting off the girl that I remember from Claire's hospital room. The girl's eyes are sunken and rimmed with dark smudges like charcoal, but these smudges won't ever rub off. A tube runs from the tank at the back of the wheelchair to the girl's nose, providing a steady stream of oxygen. She looks so tired. The way Claire looked at the end. Like breathing is too much effort. I can feel tears behind my eyes. Can see Claire sitting there instead. The little girl drags in a harsh breath and coughs, grimacing. When the cough passes she presses a hand to her lips, wiping them, and then smiles at me.

"I like your shirt." Her voice is high and thready, a faint echo of her mother's.

"Thanks," I say, glancing down. I wasn't paying attention when I grabbed a shirt from the closet this morning. It's black with a smiling cartoon bunny and the words SCHOOL PREPARES YOU FOR REAL LIFE, WHICH ALSO SUCKS. Gabe bought it for me last Christmas, and while it's not exactly my style, it did make me laugh when I first saw it.

"I have a bunny poster in my room," the girl offers. She starts coughing again, harsh, racking coughs that bend her body in half as she clutches her sides. Her dad reaches down and twists the nozzle on the oxygen tank, increasing the flow. The coughs subside.

"Emily's getting tired," the woman says, one hand clutching the back of her daughter's chair. "We need to get back to our RV."

I take a step back, nodding. "Okay. I hope she feels better." The words are out before I can stop them. The sort of stupid platitude I absolutely hated when Claire was sick. Because she wasn't ever going to feel better. What the person meant was "I don't know what to say and I want to get the hell out of here so I can stop feeling so bad that you're dying." Meaningless words. They piled up around us in the hospital, suffocating. And now they're tripping out of my mouth like a belch, horrible and loud and unstoppable.

"Emily is going to be fine. This is the hometown of miracles, after all." Emily's mom gives a brittle laugh and I can hear the edge of desperation behind it.

Emily's dad has been silent this whole time, but his frown deepens and his eyes look glassy. I don't think he believes in miracles any more than I do.

"Bye," I mutter and hurry away.

Fifteen minutes later, I'm standing at the edge of the cemetery.

Chapter Thirty-Four

Graveside Confessions

A waist-high chain-link fence surrounds the cemetery, interrupted on one side by a gate with hinges that screech. I'm not sure why the fence is here. Anyone who wants in could easily climb over, even if the gate was locked. And that flimsy little fence isn't going to keep the dead inside if the zombie apocalypse happens tomorrow.

It was morning the last time I visited Claire's grave, a year ago. Now, orangey light from the setting sun makes the tombstones look like gaudy party favors scattered over the grass. Flowers dot a few of the graves, providing bursts of color, and I can see a wilting bouquet propped beside Claire's headstone. White roses. I wish I had some blue paint so I could remake them for her.

Why am I here? Claire's gone—there's no point visiting her grave. But my feet won't obey me. Instead I open the gate, step inside, and pick my way across the grass. Claire's headstone is gray granite with her name carved in large black letters. Toward the top of the stone is a creamy white oval, like an oversized necklace pendant, with an image of a cartoon angel, head bowed in prayer and hands clasped. It's one of those sappy sweet images you see on greeting cards and seems so out of place.

I crouch beside the grave and trace my index finger over Claire's name. Sometimes it's hard to remember Claire before the cancer. Like my sister was melted down by chemicals and hospital tubes and even her memory has been erased. When I think of Claire, I see her in a hospital bed, a living skeleton with pain-filled eyes. Like the little girl I saw today.

Maybe, sometimes, living is worse. I loved Claire. I hated Claire. It's all tangled together. But I never wanted her to hurt. In the end, that's all she had, long periods of agonized lucidity and longer periods of unconsciousness when her body twitched and fingers clenched if her morphine drip wasn't high enough. That's not living, floating in a sea of pain.

Suddenly, I find it: a bright, clear memory of Claire before she was diagnosed. We'd gone down to the lake as a family, although Emmet took off with some friends in a fishing boat the moment we hit the lakeshore. Claire and I stripped down to our swimsuits and dashed in, laughing breathlessly as the cold water slapped our skin. I ducked under the water and then came up, striking out in a smooth breaststroke for a red buoy tethered two hundred feet out.

Claire yelled behind me. "Del! Wait up. I can't swim that fast."

I swam harder, until my arms and legs burned and my fingers could brush the slick sides of the buoy. I knew there was no way Claire could keep up, but I was tired of having to wait around for her all the time. She was like my slower, louder, impossible-to-shake shadow. When I swam back toward the shore, Claire was lying in wait.

She dog-paddled as fast as she could, stopped close to me, and then used both hands to send a wave of water splashing over my head. I shrieked, going vertical and treading water, pushing hair out of my eyes. I sent an answering wave back at her. But Claire had pinched her nose, prepared for it. We slapped water and splashed and acted like three-year-olds for a good ten minutes.

"Stop!" Claire begged, water dripping from the end of her nose and eyelashes. She was out of breath again, smiling. "Please!"

"Fine," I grumbled, acting like I was mad despite my own smile. I turned to swim off, but Claire grabbed my arm.

"Let's be starfish." She tightened her grip, in case I tried to pull away.

I grimaced. Starfish was a game we played when we were little and Mom had just taught us to float on our backs. We'd flip over, bellies to the air, and spread our arms and legs wide, floating until we either drifted so far apart we had to shout or the waves from passing boats and swimmers knocked us together. It was a lazy, slow, and silly game. First one to break the starfish pose lost. I wanted to swim. To move.

"Please?" Claire pleaded.

She was eleven and persistently annoying. I was too old to be playing baby games, but Claire jiggled my arm, clinging tight, and hit me with another chorus of "Please, please, please? Just for a bit."

"Okay, okay," I said.

Claire immediately flipped onto her back, smacking me with her hand as she spread her arms. I lay back as well and spread my arms as wide as I could, as if I were trying to make a snow angel in the water. And then we drifted. The sounds of the lake, laughter, splashing, the thrum of a boat motor, were muffled by the water clogging my ears.

"Pops says when we die we become stars," Claire said.

"Pops says the Easter Bunny poops out jelly beans and marshmallow eggs. He's not the best source."

"Wouldn't that be cool though?"

"Pooping out jelly beans? No, thanks."

"No," she half laughed. "Being stars. We could float right up from the lake and be starfish forever, up in the sky looking down."

Claire's outstretched fingers brushed mine. A power boat passed by, sending waves crashing against my side and shoving me into Claire. We folded at the same time, neither winning.

"All right, runt. We played. Now I'm going for a swim. Go chase some fish or something." I dunked Claire under the water and swam away before she could retaliate. A month later the first cancer bruise appeared and we never made it back to the lake as a family.

I'd forgotten about the starfish game. About Claire wanting to turn into a star and fly up into the sky. Is that where she is now? Is that what she wanted in the end?

There are moments that stay with us forever, that we keep like pictures on the wall. So many of my moments are tied to Claire. To Emmet, my mom, and my dad.

I took my family for granted, until they weren't there anymore. And when the worst had happened, instead of fighting for the family I had left and holding tight to my best friend, I folded all that pain and anger inside myself and locked everyone else out. I should have been gathering moments and now it's too late.

I rest my forehead against the gravestone and, even though I know she's not here, even though I know she can't hear me, I begin to talk. I begin with the words I should have said a year ago, but never did.

"I'm sorry. I didn't mean it. I was angry and hurt and so tired of being dragged to the hospital all the time. I just wanted my life back."

The last time I saw my sister, while she was lying in that bed like a discarded doll, already deep into a coma she'd never come out of, I didn't tell her I loved her or that I'd miss her. I didn't read her stories or sing her songs. I leaned down and whispered in her ear, "I wish you'd just die already and get it over with. You ruin everything."

My last words were filled with hate and anger and I will never have the chance to take them back. Claire, ever the perfect listener, must have taken my words to heart because she died two days later. She died because I told her to.

I press my cheek against the cold stone and cry, letting out all the hurt, the pain, and regret. I was so angry with Claire for stealing away my parents, for turning me into a shadow girl.

I give a hiccuping laugh. "You know the best part? The grand cosmic joke? You died and there wasn't any normal left. Everything fell apart. I wasn't just a shadow girl, I was erased from this world, completely invisible. I didn't know how much I loved you until you weren't here anymore. I'm sorry I was an awful sister."

Words pour out of my mouth, unstoppable. I keep talking, telling Claire everything she's missed this past year. It ends, inevitably, with the miracles. I talk about Baby Cheesus, Reverend Beaudean, and most of all, the little girl in the wheelchair. I talk so long my voice goes hoarse.

"I don't know what to do. What if that girl gets worse because she came out here? What if there are others like her? What would you do, Claire?"

229

I wait a long moment. I guess part of me is listening for an answer. But it doesn't come. At least not from Claire.

"Hey," a soft voice says behind me.

I straighten and look back, wiping my cheeks. Gabe's standing two feet away, hands shoved in his pockets, shoulders down. His gray T-shirt is covered with crease marks, like he picked it out of the laundry.

"Hey," I say in an equally quiet voice. "What are you doing out here?" How much did he hear?

Gabe shrugs, kicking at a clump of grass by his foot. "I saw you walking past and thought you might want some company. When you came in here . . . I wasn't going to bug you, but it's been half an hour and I got worried. It's gonna be dark soon."

I give him a weak smile. "I won't turn into a pumpkin when the sun sets. Or grow fangs."

"You need some more time?"

I glance back at the gravestone and press my palm next to Claire's name. "No. We're done. I just needed to say good-bye."

Gabe doesn't call me on saying something so ridiculous. Claire's been gone for a year. I had my good-byes. But this time, I feel like I'm finally letting my sister go. Maybe Claire can forgive me, wherever she is now, and maybe she can't. But I have to start forgiving myself.

"I wasn't eavesdropping," Gabe says tentatively, "but I—uh—couldn't help overhearing a bit of what you said. What girl where you talking about?"

Relief makes my knees weak. He didn't overhear my confession about the horrible things I said to Claire. The feeling only lasts a second. The darkness I've been carrying around in my gut for so long is a tiny bit lighter and it's because I let all those feelings out, even if it was just to a gravestone. I'm done hiding things. As soon as this mess is over, Gabe and I are going to sit down and have a long talk. But right now, there's something more important to discuss. I explain again about the kid, about why her family's in Clemency.

Gabe's mouth tightens and his eyes are sad. He drops down next to me, his knee brushing mine.

"If it was only Baby Cheesus, I don't think people would be dragging their sick kids to Clemency, you know?" I explain. "But they think there are all these miracles happening and maybe they'll find one too."

He sighs. "Maybe some of the miracles are real. Maybe more will be."

"Not the ones they're coming here to see. And does that whole 'ends justify the means' argument work for you? Because I figure the means matter. Especially about this. Seeing that girl, it was awful. I don't know if I can keep this secret, if I can lie to everyone we know."

"We don't have to lie to them, we just have to keep quiet. Dad said he wouldn't make any more fakes."

"It's still a lie. We're still part of it."

Gabe rubs his forehead, looking tired. "I know." His words are so low I can barely make them out. "I just wish there was some other way."

I hug him and he hugs me back, both of us squeezing tight. I want him to tell me that everything's going to be okay. But there have been enough lies. "We need to convince your dad to admit he faked the miracles."

Gabe shudders and we pull apart, sitting side by side. He draws his knees up to his chest. "I'm not turning Dad in to the police or the press."

"I'm not asking you to. Let's just talk to him, okay?"

Gabe won't meet my eyes, but he nods.

I reach over and squeeze his arm. "Can we meet at your place in an hour? There's something I have to do first." Gabe looks ready to protest, but I quickly add, "It doesn't have anything to do with the miracles. Just family stuff."

He reaches out and twines his fingers with mine, holding tight. I feel like electric currents are running under my skin. That tiny spark, the hyperawareness of Gabe that I've been fighting for months, is there in our intertwined fingers. But it's like a butterfly beating its wings against the side of a jar. When the glass shatters, I'm afraid the shards will end up hurting both of us.

"See you in an hour," Gabe says quietly. I let him go and make my way home.

Claire may be gone, but there's still a chance to fix things with Emmet.

Chapter Thirty-Five

Miracles Undone

I half expect Rust Bucket to be missing when I arrive home, but it's there in the driveway, casually leaking oil as usual. I locate my brother in his room and knock tentatively on the door, even though it's open. Emmet glances up, pulling his headphones off. He looks both annoyed and terrified. I guess that's fair; I'm feeling the same way.

I step inside and pull his door closed behind me. Emmet's room is decorated in football chic, with posters of his favorite players crowding the walls. His comforter looks like a football field, complete with end zones, and there's a pile of dirty laundry almost as tall as I am at the end of his bed.

I pick a spot that isn't contaminated with dirty socks or discarded books and plant myself, hands on hips. "You could have told me."

Emmet juts out his chin, eyes narrowing. "Told you what?"

"That you're gay." The words seem obscenely loud and Emmet flinches, eyes darting around as though a horde of reporters is going to leap out of his closet. "It doesn't make a difference, you're still my brother and I'll love you no matter what."

"I'm not—" Emmet begins, but I hold up a hand.

"Please. I saw you. That girlfriend in another city? She's a he, right?"

Emmet nods reluctantly.

"Okay. Why all the secrecy?"

"I can't just come out." Emmet looks at me like I'm dumber than dirt. "I'm a football player. I'd get kicked off the team if the other guys or coach found out."

"You wouldn't get kicked off the team, don't be stupid."

Emmet snorts. "Name one person who's gay in this entire town."

He waits, but he's right, I can't name one. "Fine. But, that doesn't mean our town is full of homophobes."

"You aren't in the locker rooms every day; you don't hear the jokes they tell or the way they make fun of celebrities who come out. Look, it's no big deal, I date the occasional cheerleader and no one suspects a thing."

"You're lying about who you are. Of course that's a big deal. You could have told me the truth, at least. Or did you think I'm just another bigot who'd make fun of you?"

"I didn't . . . I just—" He drops his gaze and stares at the carpet like there's some deep answer waiting for him in the worn fibers. "You're all I've got left," Emmet mutters finally.

That surprises me. But maybe we're not as broken as I thought. Maybe he needs me, just as much as I need him. I take a tentative step and then another, stopping in front of Emmet. He looks up at me, still sitting at his desk. Before I can overthink things, I reach down and hug him.

He's stiff at first but then he hugs me back. "I love you, no matter what," I say.

Emmet's voice is gruff when he says, "Yeah. Love you too and all that crap."

I pull away and punch him in the shoulder. "Don't worry, I still think you're an asshole."

Later, I meet Gabe in front of his house, still off-kilter from my talk with Emmet. Everything I believe and know keeps changing. I can't help worrying about what else is going to change tonight.

Gabe and I nod at each other, looking a little grim, and head inside.

Mr. Beaudean is sitting at the kitchen table, shucking peas, when we stop in the kitchen doorway. Gabe's dad looks up with a forced smile.

"Excellent. Mrs. Purdy gave me an entire sack filled with fresh pea pods and I could use some help with them."

I pull out a chair and drop heavily onto it. Gabe stays in the doorway, resting a shoulder against the doorframe.

I wait for Gabe to say something but when he doesn't I jump in, voice nervous. "We wanted to talk about the miracles."

Mr. Beaudean sighs and rests his elbows on the table, head slumping forward. "It was too much to hope the other night's conversation would satisfy you two."

"Things have gotten so crazy with the media, the miracles and everything," I begin.

Gabe finally speaks up. "People have started dragging their sick relatives to Clemency to be healed."

Mr. Beaudean's eyes sharpen on us. "What are you talking about?"

So I explain. Again. Not leaving out a single detail about the girl and her apparent situation. Mr. Beaudean shakes his head, face graying as I talk.

He drags a hand over his face, the lines in his forehead deepening. "I never meant for any of this to happen," he mutters.

"I know you think the miracles aren't hurting anyone, but they are," I say. "What if that girl gets worse because her family dragged her here instead of keeping her in the hospital on chemo?"

Mr. Beaudean shakes his head. "She might get better," he says, but the words are feeble.

"And she might not." For once I'm not yelling or shouting. I'm not letting anger or panic or pain move my mouth for me and I know what I'm saying is right. "Maybe the miracles are doing some good, but they're doing a lot of harm too. Look at what happened with Mel's mom and now this girl. Did you even realize you put that stupid well panel up on the anniversary of Claire's death? My mom has been crying herself to sleep for weeks because she thinks if Claire had just held out a year longer, Baby Cheesus would have miraculously cured her."

Mr. Beaudean looks like I've sucker punched him and his face pales. "I didn't know, Del. I'd never do anything to hurt you or Gabe."

"I know," I whisper, feeling tears threaten again. "But all of this, the lies, the miracles, they are hurting me and other people as well."

Gabe takes a step into the room, toward his dad. "If someone else came to you, someone from the congregation, and said they'd faked those miracles, what would you tell them?"

Mr. Beaudean sags in his chair like a balloon deflating in on itself. "You'll make a fine pastor one day. Smarter than your old man, anyway." He gets to his feet and shuffles over to the phone. It's an old thing, green with a cracked plastic handle and a curly cord connecting the handset to the base. Mr. Beaudean punches in a number and then lifts the handset to his ear.

"Adam?" Mr. Beaudean says. "Yeah, listen, I need you to call a city council meeting. And invite whatever press is still in town. Can you set it up for tomorrow evening?" He's quiet a minute before continuing. "I know it's asking a lot to meet on a Sunday night. Can you do it or not?" Pause. "Of course it's important. No. No, it's not another miracle. But it does concern them."

He has to be calling Mayor Thompson. The only other Adam in town runs a car wash off Main and I doubt the Suds Company is going to help any of us. From the sounds of it, Mayor Thompson isn't thrilled about Mr. Beaudean's request. But after another minute or two of wrangling he must agree because Mr. Beaudean says, "Thanks. I appreciate it. I'll see you at the meeting tomorrow."

And suddenly things are in motion. One more day before the truth comes out. One more day before Gabe's dad is in complete disgrace. I give Gabe a worried look and he grimaces back. We're doing the right thing. What we have to do. But my stomach is sick with worrying about what's gonna happen to Gabe when the truth about his dad comes out. What if Mr. Beaudean is right and they have to move?

Gabe walks to his dad and puts a hand on his arm. "Thank you."

Mr. Beaudean doesn't look up, still staring at the phone lying back in its cradle.

It's awkward being the only one sitting so I get up from the table and grip my hands together tightly. "I'll get out of your hair."

Gabe shakes his head. "Let me walk you home at least."

I nod, mumble good-bye to his dad, and scurry outside.

CHAPTER THIRTY-SIX

One Last Piece of Normal

The walk home is endless. I don't know what to do with my hands so I shove them in my front pockets, but that feels awkward too. Gabe keeps shooting little glances at me. Finally he says, "It'll be okay."

"You don't believe that." I kick a rock out of my way. It skitters over the sidewalk and smacks into the wheel of a kid's tricycle with a dull *thunk*.

"It will be okay," he insists. "In the end things will turn out like they're supposed to and whatever happens, happens."

"How can you not be freaking out? I'm freaking out and it's not my dad who's about to be run out of town."

Gabe grimaces. "Nice visual."

"You know people are going to go nuts when your dad admits to faking the miracles."

"Probably. But they'll get over it."

"And if you have to leave?"

"I can't think about that right now. I'm sorry. The past two days have majorly sucked. Can we have one last night of normal? Please?"

I'm quiet a little too long and Gabe's shoulders tense. He stops walking and I turn to face him. "I don't know what normal is anymore," I say, finally.

"It's the two of us. Just hanging together. The way it's always been."

"So you want to hang out? Go grab a slice of pizza, sit on the curb, and watch cars drive past? How can you act like nothing's changed?"

"Because not everything has."

I give him a hard look. "Really? Nothing's changed between you and me?" I feel like I swallowed a tennis ball. It's choking me and I have trouble getting the words out. Does he regret grabbing my hand earlier? Or was that a friendly gesture and I totally misread things? I feel like an idiot.

He flushes. "Okay, maybe things are a little different. But you're still my best friend. You're still the person I trust most in this world and I don't want things to be weird between us. I want to go sit by the creek and throw rocks in the water. You and me and five million mosquitoes. Our summertime ritual."

"It's fall." But I soften a little. Because he's the person I trust most in this world too. Is it so wrong to want to hang on to something normal? "Okay. You, me, and the mosquitoes. Let's go."

Gabe smiles, tentative and slow. I smile back, although it's a bit stiff. We start walking again but this time we turn away from my house, toward the little creek that runs on the east edge of town. Most of the year the creek is barely two feet across and only ankle deep. It's slow moving and lichen grows on the rocks by the bank. There are three large boulders near where the creek curves away from town, out toward the farmlands. That's where we head. A long time ago, when we were twelve, Gabe and I scratched our initials into the side of the largest boulder.

Not deep—we only had an old screwdriver—but the letters are still there, jerky and imperfect.

As I climb up onto the middle boulder, I slide my fingers over our initials. DRD. Delaney Roberta Delgado. Six inches away are Gabe's, GBB, Gabriel Beauregard Beaudean. We didn't bother adding a plus sign or BFFs 4 EVER or any of that other crap little kids write. We'd simply claimed the rock as our own. No hearts for us. The distance between our initials, the lack of any other embellishment, feels ominous tonight.

The cicadas buzz loudly in the trees around us and before long I'm slapping mosquitoes. Gabe scours the edge of the creek, gathering small stones. He piles them in a heap between the two of us when he climbs up beside me. It's dark, but the trees are sparse this close to the water and enough moonlight filters down to let us see a bit. It softens the edges of things.

We take turns tossing rocks into the creek, seeing who can make the biggest splash. Before long we're laughing. The tension slips away. I throw a stone a little too close and drops of water splash over our jeans.

"Hey!" Gabe says in mock outrage.

I laugh harder and deliberately throw another rock close by his feet. He scowls and grabs my arms, stopping me from splashing more water on him. He's suddenly too close, the playfulness gone. I look up at Gabe and he's staring back at me. I go completely still and Gabe's hands loosen on my arms, sliding around my back and pulling me even closer. His head lowers and in the next moment, we're kissing. Soft and tentative. A brush of lips on lips. I wind my arms around his neck and hold on tight. We kiss for a long time. And it's hot and sweaty and wonderful and impossible all at the same time.

When we draw apart I shiver, missing his arms around me. Gabe twists so we're sitting side by side rather than facing each other and wraps an arm around my shoulders. I rest my head against him and listen to the creek burbling lazily at our feet. Overhead, the stars go on forever, bright pinpricks, and the crickets rasp a furious chorus that can't quite drown out the thump, thump, thump of my heart beating hard against my chest.

"We need to head back," Gabe says in a ragged voice, giving my shoulders a squeeze. He clears his throat.

"Okay." But I don't move. I want to stay here, perched on this rock with his arm around me, forever. If we leave this place I'm worried we'll never come back. That it'll be like that day at the lake with Claire; a last moment of calm before our lives get tossed in a blender.

"Lots of colleges have art programs," Gabe says.

I draw away. "What's that supposed to mean?"

"It's only one more year and then we're both off to college. Lots of schools have art programs as well as architecture. We can attend the same school. So even if—" He breaks off, clearing his throat again like he can't force the words out.

"Yeah," I say. We both know his dad's right. There's a good chance Mr. Beaudean won't be allowed to stay on at Holy Cross after tomorrow's meeting with the town council. Their house belongs to the church and without a job or a place to live, they won't be staying in Clemency. Mr. Beaudean might have to move pretty far away to find a congregation willing to take on a preacher with that much scandal hanging over his head. Maybe even give up the church altogether. I might never see Gabe again. That thought hurts so bad I shove it aside. There's always email, the phone, and vid chats. It's not like he's going to disappear from my life. But he won't be here. Something with claws and teeth is hollowing out my chest, leaving an empty space. I want Gabe to kiss me again and fill it back up. "What happened just now—" I begin.

Gabe presses a finger against my lips before dropping it. "I've wanted to kiss you for a long time."

I grin. "How long?"

"Long enough," he mutters. He brushes a hand over my cheek and I shiver.

And then we're kissing again. When we finally pull back, we're both breathing hard. Gabe slides off the boulder and holds a hand out to me. I take it and we walk to my house, fingers tangled together.

Tomorrow, everything will change. Again. The media trucks will pack up and leave, Clemency's citizens will erupt with gossip and bickering, as they always do whenever anything big happens, and my world will turn inside out. But right now, Gabe's hand is in mine and the only mystery left is where the two of us are headed. I'm not sure about anything else in this world: God, tomorrow, why awful things happen. But I'm sure about Gabe and he's right, I'm going to be okay. Claire's death didn't destroy me. And maybe it didn't completely destroy my family either. I think of Mom, sitting at the table this morning with her stack of pancakes and the way she stood outside my door last night, saying she loves me. I think of Emmet and our awkward hug just hours ago. I have a chance to change things with both of them. There are as many beginnings in life as there are endings. I squeeze Gabe's hand tighter and he squeezes back.

Acknowledgments

For someone who writes novels, sometimes it's shockingly hard for me to find the right words, but I'll do my best.

Thank you a million times over to my incredible agent, Mandy Hubbard. You plucked my story from the slush pile and helped it find wings. I couldn't ask for a better agent. Even if you do occasionally send me into the deep, dark woods to gather sticks for s'mores.

Thank you to my editor, Adrienne Szpyrka, for falling in love with *Cheesus* and championing it from day one. I'm insanely lucky to have you and so glad we got to work together.

Thank you to all the writers who helped me on this crazy journey, but most especially: to Rachel Lynn Solomon for being an amazing CP, giving the best book recs, and always being ready with a virtual hug when needed; to Addie Thorley for reading my book a million times, sharing stories, silly hats, and forcing me to rap on video. I'm so blessed to have you in my life; to Kate Foster, freelance editor extraordinaire and fantastic friend—you read my novel over and over, put up with my grammar-challenged ways, and cheered louder than anyone at every tiny success; to Jennifer Park for moral support, crazy cross-country train trips, and Bigfoot hunting at Camp ECLA; to Erica B. for reading an early version of this novel and being honest.

Thank you also to the various writing and critique groups that helped with early versions of this novel, including The Private Eyes and YANA on Scribophile.

Thank you, Mom, for teaching me to love words and always pushing me to do my best. Sorry for all the cursing in this book. I promise to revive Grandma's curse jar in penance and take you out to dinner with the proceeds.

Special thanks to my husband, John: you cheered me on even when you weren't quite sure what you were cheering for. There is no one I'd rather spend my life with. Thank you for writing journals, brainstorming, chocolate milkshakes, and leaving comic books scattered around the house in an effort to lure me into reading them with you. You're a sneaky bastard and I love you. Always.

To my kids, thank you for loving books as much as Mommy and always begging for just one more story. You light up my world with your laughter, enthusiasm, and energy. You still can't read this book until you're older, but thanks for asking. Every day. Ten times.

For those who helped me along the way whose names aren't listed above, please know I'm only trying to protect your secret identities and air of mystery, but I'm still sending a huge thank you your way.

And last, but not least, to everyone who reads this book, thank you for sharing Del and Gabe's world for a little while.

About the Author

J. C. Davis checks all her food for funny pictures, but so far she's only found an Eiffel Tower–shaped Cheeto. It was delicious. In addition to writing, J. C. is an amateur photographer, runs a Harry Potter meetup group, and embraces all things nerdy. She lives in Dallas, Texas, with her husband, two kids, a pair of rowdy dogs, an incontinent cat, a hamster with a ridiculously long name, and two adorable hedgehogs who want to take over the world. *Cheesus Was Here* is her debut novel.